Also available from Diana Palmer

Wyoming Men Series

Wyoming Strong
Wyoming Bold
Wyoming Fierce
Wyoming Tough
Wyoming Rugged

Long, Tall Texans

Dangerous
Merciless
Courageous
Protector
Invincible
Untamed

The Morcai Battalion

The Morcai Battalion
The Recruit

For a complete listing of books by Diana Palmer,
please visit dianapalmer.com.

DIANA PALMER

THE MORCAI BATTALION: INVICTUS

HQN™

HQN™

ISBN-13: 978-0-373-77966-6

The Morcai Battalion: Invictus

Recycling programs for this product may not exist in your area.

To all the fine professors at Piedmont College in Demorest, Georgia, who taught me to look at the world in a new and different way. Especially to those I haven't mentioned in previous dedications who were my mentors in history and other subjects back when I was a college student in the 1990s: Dr. Ralph Singer and Dr. Al Pleysier in the history department; in anthropology, Dr. Max White; in Japanese, Dr. Jeanne White; in Spanish, Dr. Joe Palmer; and in English, Dr. William Smith, among many others.

This science fiction series also owes much to Dr. Rob Wainberg, my mentor for the biological aspects of the Cehn-Tahr (and, I rush to add, any mistakes in interpretation are my own, not his). The idea for the combination of human/Cehn-Tahr genes to restructure Ruszel was his. Hope I got it right, Rob.

This novel is also dedicated to my family: my husband, James; my son, Blayne Kyle; my daughter-in-law, Christina; my granddaughter, Selena Marie; my grandson, Donovan; my sister, Dannis, and her daughters, Amanda Belle Hofstetter and Maggie Cole; my other nieces, Helen Hunnicutt, Valerie Kyle, Kathy Thomas; my nephews, Bobby Hansen and Tony Woodall and their families; Rodney, Paul and James and all their families; my best friend, Ann Vandiver (who forced me to take all my manuscripts out of the closet and market them in the first place); my brothers-in-law, Doug Kyle and Sonny Merck; my sisters-in-law, Kathleen Woodall and Victoria Kyle; my great-nieces and great-nephews, great-great-nieces and nephews and the rest of my wonderful in-laws. And to my extended family, my readers, who keep me going with their affection and loyalty. Love you all.

CHAPTER ONE

SILENCE, MADELINE RUSZEL thought, was overrated. In the darkness, all alone, she heard nothing outside the room. It was obviously soundproof. She wondered if the Cehn-Tahr needed perfect silence in order to sleep.

The thought made her curious. Memcache, the home planet of the Cehn-Tahr, had become her home since her rescue from a crash on the planet Akaashe with her military unit. Her former Holconcom commander, Dtimun, had defied his government and her own to save her life. She was recuperating from her injuries, but also facing a new and dangerous challenge once she healed. It was hard to sleep with the most momentous decision of her life hanging over her. She was going to agree to a procedure that would change the very structure of her body, and to a mission that might mean her death.

She heard the wind stir outside. She wondered if her former commander had as much trouble sleeping as she was having. This place, this stone fortress, was his home. She was still amazed to find herself here, instead of back on the Tri-Galaxy Fleet's planet, Trimerius, where wounded military with life-threatening injuries such as hers had been were customarily hospitalized.

She hoped Dtimun wasn't in too much trouble with his government for pulling the Holconcom out of the Tri-Galaxy Fleet in order to rescue her. She, and all the humans aboard the Cehn-Tahr ship *Morcai*, were now under threat of court-martial and spacing. The Terravegan ambassador, Aubrey Taylor, had mandated the return of all human military back into Terravegan units, thus forcing the Holconcom's human component to return to its own base. The humans, all fond of Madeline, had refused to comply with the order, which also forbade any attempt to rescue her from Akaashe. So now they, and she, were fugitives from justice. She wished, not for the first time, that ambassadors had less power. They were the equivalent of world leaders in the totalitarian society to which Terravegans belonged.

She drew in a slow breath, delighted to notice that it was not as painful as before. Her injuries would have been fatal, but she'd made a friend during an earlier mission. She saved the life of an elderly Cehn-Tahr soldier. It was he who had come with the Holconcom to Akaashe to get her. It was his powerful mind that had healed her. She owed him a lot.

She shifted in the bed, restless. She wasn't used to inactivity. She'd been in the military since she was very young. At the age of eight, she'd been divisional champion marksman in the sniper company where she'd first served. Her career as a soldier had been satisfying. So had her career as a doctor, a field that paired diagnostic and surgical functions and specialties in one individual. She was an internist, dealing with Cularian racial types such as Cehn-Tahr and Rojok. She was also medical chief of staff for the Holconcom ship *Morcai*. Or she had been, until Ambassador Taylor had transferred her to a commando unit in the all-female Amazon Division and put her in harm's way.

It had been a move she hadn't fought. Her helpless

attraction to her commanding officer had resulted in a behavior he couldn't control, one which had almost cost him his career. The Cehn-Tahr had mating behaviors which were violent and quite noticeable. When a human was involved, the consequences would have been deadly. The Interspecies Act forbade any mingling of genetic material between Cehn-Tahr and non-Cularian races, such as humans. Dtimun had often hinted that the Cehn-Tahr—genetically modified to be vastly physically superior to any other race—had many feline behaviors.

Which raised a question in her mind. Did the Cehn-Tahr sleep at night, like humans, or did they subsist on catnaps? She knew they could eat small mammals whole, owing to the striated muscle in their esophagus. But they also had a detached hyoid bone. That meant that they should be able to purr, like the small cats that occupied space on Terravega. That was an interesting idea. She'd heard the commander growl. She'd heard what passed for laughter among the Cehn-Tahr. She'd never heard one of them make a purring sound. Well, just because they had the anatomical structure to make it possible didn't mean they did it, anyway. The commander had intimated that there were still secrets about the Cehn-Tahr that they'd never shared, even with their human crewmates. She wondered what they were.

She got up, a little stiffly, and walked to the window. With a soft sigh, she opened the shutter-like wings and let in the night breeze. It carried warm breezes with the scent of the same flowers that occupied pots in her bedroom. No cut flowers here, she'd noticed, and smiled as she decided that Caneese had been responsible for that. Dear Caneese, who took such good care of her. It was comforting to have a woman's touch. Especially for Madeline, who had been raised in a government nursery on Terravega.

She was so unlike Cehn-Tahr females. Madeline was independent and spirited, a capable soldier, a competent doctor. Cehn-Tahr women were forbidden to join the military at all, much less operate as combat soldiers. It had been a point of contention between Madeline and Dtimun. Their battles had become the stuff of legends. And now she was living in his home, about to be bonded with him in preparation for the creation of a hybrid child. The pregnancy would act as a disguise to gain them entrance to the most notorious den of thieves in the three civilized galaxies. And they would do this, risking execution from their respective governments, to save the life of an enemy military commander. All because a traveler from the future, Komak, had told them that civilization would perish if the Rojok Field Marshal Chacon was removed from his position by the murderous Rojok head of state. It was a frightening concept, that the future could depend on a human female and an alien male and a child that Madeline was still not certain was even a possibility.

She wondered how Komak planned to do the genetic manipulation that would make her strong enough that Dtimun could mate with her without killing her. Probably by injection, she decided, using a biological catalyst to facilitate the combination of human and alien DNA. It was an intriguing scientific theory put to practical use, if he could pull it off. But why not? The Rojoks had developed similar tech, and her Terravegan former captain, Holt Stern, was proof of it. She'd seen him take on Komak and fight him to a draw.

Not that she planned on trying to deck the CO. She had considered it the day before, listening to him scoff at emotion. But, then, he had good reasons for his opinion. How terrible, to lose the one woman he'd ever cared about so violently.

She recalled their discussion about the way Cehn-Tahr marked their mates, about the aggression of mating. She would have to mate with the alien commander, if they were to assure the future timeline. A disturbing prospect, but Komak, who was from the future, had insisted that the mission was vital. Pregnancy would be part of their disguise. In all of history, no Cehn-Tahr had ever mated with a human female. It had been considered impossible, due to the uncanny physical strength of the aliens.

It was unsettling to a woman who had spent her entire life as a neuter. She had no idea what to expect, except for what she knew from a medical standpoint. Probably, she decided, it was better not to think too much about it until she had to.

"Why are you out here alone at this hour?"

She jumped at Dtimun's voice. She hadn't heard him approach.

"I couldn't sleep, sir," she stammered.

He was wearing robes, not his familiar uniform. He appeared somber and out of sorts. He moved to her side, looking out over the dark silhouettes of the trees and distant mountains. "Nor could I."

She leaned on the balcony that ran around the porch. "I'm sorry I was rude, earlier."

"I was rude first."

She laughed to herself, picturing an altercation earlier between her female physician colleague and a Cehn-

Tahr officer during which Dr. Edris Mallory had ended up with a pot of soup poured over her head.

"What?"

"I was remembering poor Edris Mallory, covered in soup."

He laughed, too. "I must confess that I can understand what motivated Rhemun to retaliate after she threw a soup ladle at him. The only thing that saved you in the past from the same fate was the lack of soup at an appropriate time."

"I know I get on your nerves," she said without looking at him. "I don't mean to."

The soft, high trill of some night bird filled the silence between them.

"I used to come here late at night when I was a child," he remarked. "There was a myth about a small winged creature with human features that fed on *entots* fruit. It grows here, in the garden. I escaped my parents and prowled, hunting. I never found the creatures."

"Every child should have access to myths," she said in a soft, dreamy tone. "My childhood was an endless series of close quarter drills and weapons instruction from the time I was old enough to stand."

He turned and scowled down at her.

In the darkness, his cat eyes gleamed neon-green. She caught her breath and jumped before she could squelch the giveaway reaction.

He wasn't offended. He only laughed. "Almost three years, Ruszel," he remarked, "and you still have not lost your fear of me in the darkness."

"I'm very sorry, sir," she said miserably. "It's just reaction. I can't help it. I'm not afraid of you. Not really."

His eyes narrowed as he saw her, quite clearly, in the

dark. "A polite lie," he concluded from her expression. "And if you bond with me, there will be new nightmares. You may gain a fear of me which you will never lose as long as you live."

"I'm a combat veteran, sir," she reminded him.

"War is familiar to you. I am not."

"We've served together for…"

"You have seen the soldier, not the hunting male," he said very quietly. "There is a vast difference in the two. Some females have renounced bonding altogether because of their fear of it."

"Sir, it can't be all that different from the way humans…join."

He looked away. "Do you think so?"

"I have studied Cularian anatomy," she pointed out. "Including Cehn-Tahr."

"From information we provided."

She had a sinking feeling in her stomach. "Sir?"

He was staring out over the darkened landscape. Silvery creatures with luminous bodies in neon blues and greens alighted on flowers, poignantly beautiful in the light of the two moons of Memcache.

"There are still secrets we keep from you, Ruszel," he said.

She was recalling things. The true strength of the Cehn-Tahr, which he revealed to her so long ago in his office. The weight of him, when he rescued her from a fall off the cliff, odd considering the streamlined outline of his tall body. The comments he made about the terror the Cehn-Tahr kindled in enemies. The fear of the Cehn-Tahr, seemingly out of proportion to what Madeline and the other humans knew of their alien crewmates.

"Your mind is busy," he commented.

"It's like trying to see through smoke, sir," she mused. "Or mirrors."

"Smoke and mirrors. An apt analogy. We are not what we seem; especially those of my Clan."

"Why do you keep so many secrets?"

He turned, letting her see his eyes, gleaming green in the darkness. "Out of selfishness, perhaps. If you do not know everything about us, you are less likely to be uncomfortable with us. We are fond of our human companions," he said simply.

"Fond?"

"You have traits that we find admirable," he continued. "Courage and tenacity and devotion to duty. For such a fragile species, you are indomitable."

She smiled. "Thanks."

He narrowed his eyes as he studied her. "We will risk much, if we go to Benaski Port."

"We will risk more if we don't go," she replied. "I for one would love to see the war end in my lifetime. Without the Rojok Field Marshal, Chacon, to fight the madness of his tyrannical government, that might not happen."

"I agree."

"Do Cehn-Tahr sleep at night, sir?" she asked abruptly.

He laughed. "Why ask such a question?"

"Because I've never really seen any of you sleep," she pointed out. "Even at *Ahkmau*, the Rojok prison camp, the only reason you slept was because I knocked you out with drugs." She pursed her lips, frowning. "And those microcyborgs, the ones you said gave you such superior strength…"

"What about them?"

"Why would you need artificial boosters for the strength you already have?"

"You see too much, Ruszel."

"Or not enough. Depending on your point of view. For instance, the readings I get for your anatomical makeup are quite frequently at conflict with what I learned in medical school."

"Imagine that," he mused.

"You have a detached hyoid bone," she persisted.

He moved a step closer. His eyes that, in the light, could change color to mirror mood, began to take on an odd glitter. "And you wonder if the Cehn-Tahr can purr?"

Her heart jumped. "I…wouldn't have put it in exactly those words."

"We have many feline characteristics, none of which we ever share with outworlders."

She backed up a step. It wasn't his manner so much as his posture that suddenly started to set off alarms in her brain. He moved like a stalking cat, silently, with exquisite grace, with a singularity of purpose that was chilling.

"To answer your first question, we do not sleep at night, as humans do. We nap at odd times during the day. At night," he added in a soft, deep tone, "we hunt."

"Hunt, sir?" She backed up another step.

He was amusing himself. His eyes were twinkling. "To answer the second question, we can control the output of your computers and the information disseminated through your military medical corps. We are not what we seem. Nor, as you guessed, do I require the microcyborgs to augment my natural strength."

She backed up one more step.

"As to the last question," he said, bending down. "Yes, we do purr. When we mate."

It had just occurred to her that they were alone and she remembered, almost too late, the effect he had on her. He was attractive to her even when she was afraid of him. Her body was reacting now, pouring out pheromones, saturating his senses. And she had no genetic modifications. Not yet. If she provoked him, here, where they were alone, she would die.

"In an instant," he gritted, and a low, soft growl issued from his throat.

"Oops," she murmured. She was measuring the distance from the balcony to a locked door and wondering if she could outsprint him when a voice broke the silence.

"This is very unwise. Very, very unwise," Caneese said, clicking her tongue in a most human manner as she joined them on the balcony. The commander stopped, dead, and turned to face her, straightening slowly.

"You know, I was just thinking the very same thing," Madeline replied quickly. She eyed Dtimun, who looked decidedly uncomfortable. "I don't really think I could outrun him."

Dtimun took longer to react as he fought down his need. He let out a long breath and glanced at Madeline. "I must agree," he told her. He smiled at Caneese. "You arrived at an opportune moment."

"As I see." She moved between them. "It is not kind of you to frighten Madeline," she chided.

He recovered his equilibrium and laughed softly. "She has the heart of a galot," he said unexpectedly, referring to a species of giant cat. "I would never expect her to be afraid of anything. Not even me."

Madeline grinned. "At least I haven't thrown things at you," she added, alluding to their earlier conversation about Rhemun and Edris Mallory.

"A lie," he said with a flash of green eyes. "Once, when I refused to let you treat a wound on my leg, you threw a piece of medical equipment at me."

"It wasn't anything heavy or dangerous," she pointed out.

"Should I ask why the two of you were out here?" Caneese asked.

"I couldn't sleep," Madeline confessed.

"I heard her outside," Dtimun added. "There are dangers at night, even here in the fortress."

"Yes," Caneese said, but more gently. She smiled at Madeline. "You should never come out here alone at night. Or with him," she added mischievously, indicating Dtimun with a faint nod of her head. "He is more dangerous than anything you might discover in the dark."

"I was just noticing that," Madeline murmured drily.

He gave her a long, searching look.

"The ceremony must be soon," he said to Caneese in Cehn-Tahr, in the familiar tense. "And Ruszel's transformation must be even sooner."

"Komak has everything ready to proceed early tomorrow," Caneese replied. "I will conduct the bonding ceremony myself, but it must be witnessed."

"It is only a temporary measure," he began uncomfortably.

"It must be witnessed," she replied firmly. "I cannot explain. You must trust me."

He let out a rough sigh. "You risk much."

"You risk more, by keeping secrets from her." She

moved closer to him, aware of Madeline's curiosity. She dared not satisfy it. "Dtimun, you must tell her the truth."

"No."

"She will see it for herself, when you mate," she persisted.

"We will conduct the pairing in total darkness," he said, evading her eyes. "I will make sure that she does not see me. She will not know."

Caneese frowned worriedly. "Our laws require that we use no artificial means of camouflage during a bonding ceremony. How will I explain that to the witnesses?"

He cocked his head. "You will find a way around that," he said with affection.

She shook her own head. "You presume too much."

"I do not." He bent and laid his forehead against hers. "It will change everything, once she knows," he said bitterly. "I do not wish it to happen. Not yet." He lifted his head. His eyes were sad and reflective. "She plans to have a memory wipe. The child will be regressed. She will go back to the Holconcom and remember nothing. But I will have the memory of it. Of her. I do not wish to remember her distaste."

"You underestimate the intensity of her feelings for you," Caneese said simply.

He laughed shortly. "Do you not remember the one time we revealed ourselves to a party of humans, during the Great Galaxy War?"

She grimaced. "They were primitive humans…"

He turned away. "I will not risk it."

She didn't press him. It would have done no good.

He was too much like her. Neither of them would retreat from a decision, once made.

"The bonding will take place tomorrow, after Komak's genetic manipulation, Madeline," Caneese told her gently. "Are you certain that you are rested and healed enough for the procedure?"

"I'm just sore and a little weak," Madeline assured her with a smile. "We don't have a lot of time, if we're to save Chacon and the princess." Both the enemy commander and the Cehn-Tahr princess had recently gone missing.

"I still do not like it," the older woman said solemnly. "It is a very great risk."

Madeline moved closer to her. "I'll be the commander's eyes and ears," she said softly. "He'll be all right."

Dtimun's eyebrows shot up almost to his hairline. "You presume to protect me from harm?" he asked in a hopelessly arrogant fashion.

Madeline grinned at him. "I always try my best to protect you, sir. I'll remind you that when we were in *Ahkmau…*"

"Not again," he groaned.

Caneese laughed out loud. "What is this, about *Akhmau*?"

"I operated on him under battlefield conditions when he went prematurely into the *dylete*," she recalled smugly, reminding Caneese of an earlier conversation. She frowned. "Well, in one stage of it, anyway. Can you still call it the time of half-life when it's only one of many?" she added thoughtfully.

"Call it what you like," Dtimun said gruffly. "I am going to bed."

"You sleep well, sir," Madeline said. "If I hear anything threatening outside, I'll attack it for you."

He muttered something under his breath, turned on his heel, and stalked back across the balcony.

Caneese was grinning, overcome with mirth. "I have never seen him in such a state," she chuckled.

"I get on his nerves," Madeline said, grinning back. "It keeps him on his toes. He does tend to brood."

"Yes. Even as a child, he was like that."

"You've known him that long?" Madeline asked.

Caneese's eyes softened. "I have." She studied the younger woman quietly. "You are uneasy about the bonding. You have never known the touch of a hunting male."

Madeline's heart jumped. She averted her eyes. Uneasy was an understatement.

"You must not dwell on it," Caneese said. "But you must use your strongest sedative. You are frightened of him in the darkness already. This will augment it."

Madeline flushed. "His eyes glow…"

"We have feline eyes," Caneese reminded her.

She frowned. "He said something curious. He said that you keep more secrets than we know, and that you aren't what you seem."

"There have been incidents, in the past," Caneese said carefully. "When humans…"

"Stop there," came a commanding voice into her mind. "Say no more to her."

Caneese grimaced. "Well, it is nothing that concerns you," she amended. She smiled. "You should try to rest. Tomorrow will be stressful."

Madeline hesitated. "What is it like?" she asked, the words almost torn out of her.

Caneese only smiled. "You will understand soon."

Madeline sighed and turned away. "I suppose so. Good night."

"Sleep well." Caneese bit her lower lip as she watched the fragile human female walk away. Madeline was concerned, but Caneese did not dare satisfy the other woman's curiosity. She hoped that Madeline could summon enough nerve not to run, as she had tried to, just before her own first mating. It was not a memory she liked to revisit, despite the pleasure of the ones that followed.

KOMAK HAD USED a curious mixture, which contained bone marrow cells and Cehn-Tahr DNA, as well as an accelerant whose properties he would not disclose, to facilitate Madeline's transformation into a human with the strength of the aliens with whom she had served for almost three years. After he finished with the initial procedure, he injected another mixture into the artery at Madeline's neck with a laserdot. "You must not be nervous," he said gently. "I assure you, I know what I am doing."

She managed a smile for him. "For a time-traveling magician, you're not bad, Komak."

He chuckled. "So I am told."

She studied his face. "You know, you do use human facial expressions more than any Cehn-Tahr I've ever known."

"You are remembering the traces of human DNA in my blood, when you typed and cross-matched it to transfuse the commander at *Ahkmau*."

"Yes."

He removed the laserdot placer. "We all keep secrets. That one must remain my own."

"The commander and I think you're related to someone who lived in this time period."

"You are both astute. I am."

"Can you tell us who?"

He smiled and shook his head. "That is one subject we must not visit."

"Do you have human DNA, or was it just a glitch in my equipment, as I thought at the time?"

He put down the laserdot and looked her in the eye. "Answer your own question. Do I resemble a human?"

She sighed. "No, Komak," she had to admit, smiling. "You look like the rest of your species."

He was amused. She did not know the true tech he employed, although he had let her think she did, and he had no intention of telling her. To do so might reveal too soon the secret Dtimun kept from her. He smiled back. "We are all one color, one race. Unlike you humans, who come in all colors and races."

"There's a legend that my people were once all tea-colored," she recalled.

He pursed his lips. He didn't speak.

She frowned. "You know something. Tell me."

"Your race was once tea-colored, as you say, from millennia of racial mixing. Humans rose to become a great space-faring civilization. Then a comet collided with your planet of origin and reduced your species to a gene pool of less than ten thousand," he said simply. "The reduction mutated you, so that the old genetic material was reborn and you split, once more, into separate races and coloring. Your leaders discovered relics of this civilization, but they hid it quite carefully."

"Hid it? Why?" she asked, exasperated.

"Would you reveal to an optimistic, ambitious population with growing tech ability that another civilization had risen to such heights, only to be destroyed in a natural catastrophe?"

She thought about that. "I don't know."

"It would diminish your accomplishments, dull your ambition," he suggested. "It would limit the achievements."

"I suppose it might. How did you come to be a time traveler?" she asked. "And who discovered its potential?"

He grinned. "It was me. Building on tech developed by one of my...antecedents," he said carefully, "I perfected the ability to jump through dimensions, into different time lines."

"But how?"

"I cannot say. But the Nagaashe are the key," he added. He sobered. "You made the discovery possible, by convincing them to trade with us. You do not yet realize the scope of that accomplishment. It will lead to untold discoveries."

"I just crashed on their planet," she said softly.

He shook his head with awe. "I read about this period of history. But the records were quite scant, and frankly the first-person accounts of it were grossly understated. All of you were too modest about your actions. And nowhere was it recorded that Chacon himself assisted in your rescue. Or your...old fellow," he added. "There were whispers, of course, but they were dismissed as myths."

She smiled. "I make odd friendships."

He chuckled. "Indeed you do. I am most proud to be

included in them," he said gently. "You and the commander are more than I ever realized from my research. The two of you have been a constant delight." He drew in a long breath as he looked at her. "Serving with you is my greatest honor and privilege." His eyes saddened. "I will miss you both."

"Miss us?"

He nodded. "I must leave. Today."

"Today? Surely not before the bonding ceremony!"

"Yes." His face tautened. "I must not interfere in any way with this timeline." His eyes were soft with affection. "It is precious. More precious than I can tell you." His face tautened. "There is another matter," he said quickly. "You must not return to the Amazon Division, for any reason. Do you understand? It is important."

Her heart jumped. "Komak, this is only for a mission," she said. "I can't tell you what it is, except to say that many lives may depend on its success. But afterward, whatever happens, I will go back to duty." She averted her eyes. "I've already spoken to Strick Hahnson about doing a short-term memory wipe on me. I won't remember anything…"

"Memories are precious, Madelineruszel," he said quietly. "Your feelings for the commander are quite intense. Do you really want to forget them?"

Her sad eyes met his. "He's an aristocrat. I'm just a grunt of a soldier, and I'm human. He must…bond with a woman of his own species, to produce an heir who can inherit his estates." She lowered her gaze to the table. "He feels nothing for me. I just get on his nerves. And right now, he's locked into a behavioral cycle that could cost him his life or his career, all because of my intense feelings. I have to do whatever I can to save him. Whatever the cost. I can't go back to the Holconcom," she added quickly, conspiratorially. "Don't you see? Even with a memory wipe, I might feel the same for him, all over again, and trigger the same behavior. I won't put him at risk a second time."

Komak's face was grim. "You care so much?"

"I care so much," she said huskily.

"But, if there is a child, as I feel certain there will be…" he began hesitantly.

"The child can be regressed. It's a gentle process. He'll be absorbed back into the tissues of my body." She didn't look at him. "Nobody must know. It would hurt his career, if it became known that he'd fathered a child onto a human female. It would…disgrace him."

"Surely he did not say that to you!"

She didn't speak. He hadn't. Not in so many words. But she knew he must have thought about their differences in status. Her jaw tautened. "I'll do whatever I need to do, for this mission to succeed. Then he'll go back to his command, I'll go back to mine. We'll be quits."

Komak looked devastated. This was not the history he had read. Surely the timeline was not so corrupted already?

"We don't always get what we want in life," she said thoughtfully. "I would have liked to keep the memory." She drew herself up to her full height. "But I'll do what's best."

He stood up, too. He moved close to her, his eyes wide and quiet and tender. "I will never forget these years with you," he said softly. "It has been an honor, to know you as a comrade."

She smiled sadly. "It has been for me, too, Komak." She shifted. "I feel...odd."

"Odd, how?" he asked, but he was smiling.

She reached impulsively for a metal sphere on the desk and closed her fingers around it. No human could have made a mark on it. She crushed it in her hand. She gasped.

He chuckled. "So. We need not ask if the experiment was a success."

She looked at the misshapen lump on her palm and laughed with delight. "No. We need not ask!"

CHAPTER TWO

MADELINE WAS A combat surgeon. She certainly knew about the reproductive process, in animals and humans, even in Rojoks. But trying to get any information about Cehn-Tahr matings was like pulling stones out of a vacuum.

She thought Caneese was the obvious person to ask. Although Caneese was very polite, she was almost mute on the subject.

"You will cope," she told Madeline gently. "The thing to remember is that you must…yield, and let nature take its course," she said finally, after searching for just the correct word.

"Yield."

"Exactly! I am so glad that we had this talk. You will feel better about the encounter, now, yes?" And she walked away, smiling.

Madeline ground her teeth into her lower lip. "Smoke and mirrors," she said to herself, nodding.

IN THE END, there was only one person she felt comfortable talking about it with and that was her partner for the event.

She found him standing on a stone patio, his hands behind him, watching the sun set over the distant mountains.

He heard her footsteps and turned. In the robes he wore at Mahkmannah, he was like a stranger. She wore robes, too, of course, but was less comfortable in them.

"You have concerns," he mused as she approached.

"Yes. Nobody will talk to me about it," she said irritably. "They talk around it."

He gave her a long look. "You must remember that women in my culture are not as self-possessed and independent as you are. We have traditions that have existed for millennia."

"I'm not denigrating your culture," she said. "I just want to know what's going to happen."

He raised an eyebrow and gave her a look of mock astonishment.

She actually blushed. "I wish you wouldn't do that," she gritted.

He laughed softly. "It is irresistible. The brawling, insubordinate medical chief of staff who sends her underlings running for cover, reduced to blushes and confusion about a process so basic that it is familiar even to children."

She glared at him. "I might remind you that I've spent the past twenty-nine years of my life as a neuter, basically without gender," she said curtly. "I've never felt…well…the sort of things women feel with men. With males. I mean…" She couldn't find the words.

He turned and moved closer, so that he could look down at her face. His hand came up and touched her red-gold hair lightly. "Madeline, you are making much work of a natural process."

She sighed. "Sir, can't you just tell me, soldier to soldier, what I'm expected to do? Caneese is the only Cehn-Tahr woman I could have asked, and she said that it was only necessary to yield and endure it." She shook her head. "Is that what the women of your culture do? Simply...yield?"

He cocked his head. "You have seen few young Cehn-Tahr women, but you spent some time with Princess Lyceria. You have also been exposed to Dacerian women. Do you notice a similarity in comportment?"

"Yes," she replied. "They're very docile, gentle females. Intelligent, but not assertive."

"Exactly."

"Then they...simply submit."

"Yes."

She frowned. It troubled her. "Wouldn't such a docile sort of female tend to exaggerate the violence of an encounter if she didn't, well, participate in it so much as endure it?"

One eyebrow went up.

She grimaced. "I'm sorry. I'm finding it difficult to explain what I mean. It's complicated to discuss something so intimate with you."

"Indeed. You and I have engaged in many verbal battles over the years, but our encounters have been nonphysical. This one will be."

She searched his eyes, looking for any sign of what he was thinking. "What do you expect of me, sir?" she asked in a soft, uncertain tone. "What is it like?"

The question, added to the sudden burst of pheromones exuding from her body when he stared at her, kindled a helpless reaction. His face tautened. Like a snake striking, his hand shot out and suddenly grasped her long hair at her nape and jerked, pulling her face up to his. The eyes stabbing into hers were jet-black. "It is like this," he said in a voice which sounded so alien that at first it was barely recognizable. It was similar to the sound a cat might make when it was angry, except with words instead of hisses. His head bent, so that his eyes filled the world, and the pressure of his hand forced her body close to his in an arc, thrilling and frightening at the same time.

Her heart jumped up into her throat. He seemed, for the first time in their long relationship as commanding officer and subordinate, so alien that she almost didn't recognize him.

"You begin to understand," he whispered, in that same odd tone, and for a split second, in a flash of presence like the blinking of a light, he seemed to be taller, far more massive than he looked. She must be hallucinating, she thought.

Her hands flattened against his robes, feeling the strength and warmth of his chest under them.

"I am not what I seem," he said.

She was a little intimidated, but she didn't let it show. She nodded. "I know. My instruments and my senses don't coincide." His eyes changed color yet again, to a burnished gold, almost glowing. She didn't know what it meant.

His hand lessened its pressure on her hair and became oddly caressing. "Weakness is prey. It invites brutality. Do you understand that?"

Her lips parted. "The more a female yields control, the more a male exercises it."

He nodded. His gaze dropped to her throat, softly vulnerable at the angle. "We are a passionate species," he whispered, bending his head. His mouth opened and slid over her throat. She felt the faint edge of his teeth. Even they felt different than they looked, different than her instrument readings described them. The slow rasp of them against the vulnerable skin of her throat should have been frightening. It was only exciting. Her heart began to race.

His nostrils splayed as stronger pheromones rushed up into them. "Delicious," he rasped. And suddenly his tongue slid over the soft flesh, abrasive and stimulating.

Her nails stabbed into his chest and she gasped audibly.

He laughed.

She was alive as she'd never been alive, on edge, shivering with sensation and curiosity. He lifted his head and looked into her eyes. His own narrowed. His chin lifted arrogantly. He looked at her as if she already belonged to him. She recalled that expression from earlier, non-physical encounters and realized that he had been possessive of her for a long time.

"We are a warrior culture," he said in a deep, velvety tone. "We conquer. For generations, our women have been taught that submission to the violence is the only way to survive it."

Her breath was coming in little spurts. "Is that why they're so afraid of it?"

"Yes. They dread the onset of the mating ritual, because they fear the aggression of the male. They have been taught that it is not feminine to meet passion with passion."

She was seeing things she'd been blind to. His calm demeanor was a front. He could control his actions, except when he was exposed to Madeline's involuntary pheromones. What she was seeing now was the true male, the true creature, without the veneer of civilized conduct.

"That is essentially correct," he said curtly. His hand contracted again on her hair and brought her face very close to his, so that she could almost taste his clean breath in her mouth. "I have forced a change in the protocols. The mating will take place in total darkness."

Her senses were heightened, but the odd statement kindled her curiosity. "Doesn't it usually?"

"No," he said flatly. "It is an innovation." He couldn't bring himself to tell her why.

He stared down at her with mingled concern and hunger. Her taut features betrayed her fear, even as she tried to hide it from him in her mind. "You are already afraid of my eyes in the absence of light. Added to that, you will experience the violence that goes with the feline response to desire." His voice rasped. "I cannot control it."

"I know that. Your eyes startle me at night. But I'm not afraid of you. Not really."

"You know that I will not hurt you deliberately."

"Of course," she said simply.

His hand contracted harshly. "But remember this," he said in a harsh, alien voice. "If you bend your neck to my teeth, I will make you pay for it!"

Her neck. If she bent her neck to his teeth. She suddenly remembered something from her biology courses. The great male cats of the human planets mated from behind. Did the Cehn-Tahr, as well?

His face lowered and his cheek rubbed hard against hers. At the same time, he lifted her and pushed her against the stone wall, pressing her there with the weight of his powerful body. She became aware of gigantic size and strength, despite her reengineered body.

The familiar commander was suddenly someone else, something else.

"You are mine," he whispered roughly at her ear, and pressed harder against her.

His mouth opened on her throat, warm and feverish and exciting. She caught her breath and shivered at the sudden rush of sensation.

He growled. The sound she made, involuntarily, sent him over the edge.

She shivered as a wave of pleasure washed over her, dulling her senses, robbing her of resistance. It was almost familiar. It came again, violent this time, so piercing and sweet that she moaned as she felt him move against her. Her nails dug into his long back hungrily as she waited for whatever came next…

"What are you doing?" Caneese demanded belligerently as she approached them. "You are not allowed to touch her before the bonding ceremony!"

He was so far gone that he growled at Caneese.

She cuffed him hard enough that the sound echoed. She growled, too. Madeline, almost mindless with her own responses, barely registered that Dtimun obeyed the older woman at once. He let go of Madeline and moved back, grasping at control and dignity.

"It is all right," Caneese told him gently. She touched his cheek lightly. "It is all right."

Madeline was getting her breath back. She was flushed. "I'm sorry," she told Caneese. "It was my fault. I only wanted to know what was going to happen."

Caneese smiled at her. "There is no need to apologize. I understand."

"The bonding ceremony is tomorrow, anyway," Madeline began.

"Yes, but the mating must be witnessed, that is the law," the older woman said gently.

Madeline had heard that odd phrasing before, but never thought about it until now. Witnessed?

Dtimun had recovered. His head bowed slightly, in deference to Caneese's position. "We were discussing certain…aspects…of the ceremony," he said with a straight face. "Madeline was curious."

Caneese's eyes were wide and shocked. "And you were telling her?"

He moved forward, took Caneese's face in his hands and, smiling, touched his forehead to hers. "I was not," he lied. "She wanted reassurance. Our customs are disturbing to her. I was attempting to explain them when things got out of hand."

"A little out of hand," Madeline said blithely. The look she gave Dtimun, unseen by Caneese, was wicked enough to make his eyes flash green.

Caneese melted. She touched Dtimun's cheek with her hand. "I had to interfere. But you must not tell her anything further. I do not want you to make her more frightened."

"Not to worry," Madeline quipped. "I've had all my shots, and I'm experienced in six martial arts."

Dtimun burst out laughing. Caneese stared worriedly from one of them to the other.

"We will not embarrass you," Dtimun assured her. He hesitated. Madeline's reaction to him was extremely stimulating. "We will not deliberately embarrass you," he corrected. "It might be…wise—" he considered his choice of words "—to double the mute screen in the mating chamber, however."

Caneese now looked horrified.

Dtimun held up a hand. "She has been known to throw things at me when she lost her temper," he said quickly, looking for an explanation that would not disturb Caneese.

"Wouldn't it be easier just to remove the ceramics from the room, sir?" Madeline asked him cheekily.

"Sir?" Caneese echoed. "Madeline, you must refrain from addressing him so."

"Sorry," Madeline replied with a smile. "Habit."

"You must consider that this is the lesser of two evils," Dtimun agreed. "She has, at least, refrained from saluting me."

"Oh, I rarely do that," she said. "In fact, we have this new guy, the *kelekom* tech, Jefferson Colby, that the commander stole…excuse me, borrowed," she added when Dtimun glared at her, "from Admiral Lawson. Colby saluted the CO so often that he was getting a crick in his neck. So we told him that we never salute the CO because it affects his ego. Right, sir?" she asked Dtimun with a grin.

He glared at her. "When we are at Benaski Port, if you refer to me as 'sir' in front of possible spies, even your pregnancy will not be enough to ward off suspicion that we are enemy agents."

"Point taken. Sorry, sir. I mean…" She hesitated. "Well, what the hell am I supposed to call you, then?" she asked.

"Madam!" he gritted.

"Madeline!" Caneese echoed.

Madeline threw up her hands. "I give up. I'm never going to be able to pull this off. I mean, look at…?"

She stopped, fascinated, as Rognan came dashing toward her as fast as his injured leg would allow.

"You must deal with this," Caneese told Dtimun helplessly. "He has been told that he will not be permitted at the ceremony. He is very upset."

"But why can't he be?" Madeline asked.

"Because he considers you his mate," Dtimun said with a flash of green eyes. "We would never make it past him into the mating chamber."

"And when she becomes pregnant, there will be no place where she can go without him," Caneese groaned, missing Madeline's flush. "He will consider the child his, as well."

"Meg-Ravens are quite fascinating to study," Dtimun mused as the bird came closer. "It is best to do it at long-range however," he sighed.

Rognan paused in front of them and flapped his wings angrily. "Rognan must come to ceremony. Rognan is family!" he muttered.

Madeline reached out and stroked his feathered head, scratching it gently. He calmed at once.

"Yes, Rognan is family," she agreed gently. "But there will be many people, and you don't like strangers around you. Yes?"

He hesitated. He ruffled his feathers. "Strangers make Rognan nervous," he agreed.

"So you can watch from a closed vid screen," she suggested, pointedly looking at Caneese.

The elder Cehn-Tahr nodded. "That will be possible."

Rognan sighed. "Very well."

Impulsively Madeline hugged him. "You must stop worrying so much about things. It isn't good for you."

He enveloped her with a huge black wing. "Rognan will try. Rognan is happy that you will be family," he added in a hesitant tone.

She drew back and smiled at him. "Thank you. That's very nice of you to say."

"You have amazing skills in diplomacy," Caneese remarked when Rognan had hobbled away. "They may be quite useful one day."

"They already are, when dealing with some individuals," she said, and glanced wickedly at her commanding officer.

He chuckled.

"What sort of witnessing are we talking about?" Madeline asked suddenly. She hadn't wanted to bring it up, but it was disturbing.

"We require proof of parentage in, shall we say, our aristocratic circles," Caneese explained solemnly. "The first mating requires witnesses."

She gaped at the aliens. "You mean people are going to stand around and WATCH us...?"

Dtimun burst out laughing at her expression.

"No, of course not," Caneese assured her quickly. "There will be a closed chamber with guards at the single entrance, to ensure that everything is correct and that only the two of you enter the room. So that there is no doubt of the child's parentage."

"But I thought that was a tradition only in royal families, when an heir was involved," Madeline said thoughtfully. "And besides," she added solemnly, "this child is temporary." She didn't add that she was quite uncertain if a child was even possible, unless Komak had put something quite unusual into that injection he'd given her. Even her Medicomp was unable to analyze its contents.

"We must follow the law, even in covert circumstances," Caneese said gently.

Madeline sighed. "I suppose so."

Dtimun walked along with them back toward the fortress. "Sfilla has arranged transport and facilities on Benaski Port. We will wait only until the pregnancy is sufficiently visible to leave." He glanced at Madeline, who looked as uncomfortable as he felt. "There is another matter. What if it is impossible for us to breed?"

"Komak assured me that it was not," Caneese interjected. "And that this first mating will bear fruit. Now let us worry no more about it," she told them firmly. "I have had a meal prepared. We can discuss the details of your journey while we eat."

Madeline followed them inside, more confused than ever. She hoped she wouldn't disgrace herself.

She glanced at the commander with a slight frown, her mind full of his behavior earlier. She was just beginning to realize that she didn't know him at all.

CHAPTER THREE

MADELINE WAS IMPRESSED by the number of guards and the obvious wealth and prestige of the guests who attended the ceremony. She wore simple robes in a pale blue gossamer fabric, her hair left long and clean and flowing in red-gold waves down her back.

Beside her, Dtimun also wore robes, similar to the ones he'd worn to the Altair embassy when he'd blackmailed her into accompanying him. She had to restrain a smile, remembering some of their earlier battles.

He glanced down at her with twinkling green eyes, amused at her thoughts. She curbed them. It really wasn't a time to be humorous.

Caneese herself officiated at the brief ceremony. She welcomed the guests, who seemed to be shocked about some aspect of the affair, and joined Dtimun and Madeline at a small altar at one end of the spacious chamber.

She instructed them to join hands. Then she read the ceremony in High Cehn-Tahr, the ancient tongue of her people. Madeline barely understood a word of it. She was far more aware of her surroundings and the experience to come, apprehension having kept her sleepless. She had taken Caneese's advice and used a sedative. But it wasn't doing much good.

In a heartbeat, the ceremony was over and Caneese was smiling at them. She nodded.

Dtimun glanced at Madeline and indicated the back of the room. She followed him, aware of the silence as they left the guests behind.

He didn't look at her as they approached a door guarded by two Cehn-Tahr soldiers in full dress uniform. The guards stared straight ahead, their eyes never deviating to the bonded pair.

One guard touched a switch and the door to the suite opened. Madeline went in, followed by Dtimun, and the door closed behind them. It was pitch-black inside. The only sound was a sudden, deep growl emanating from her companion. It was reminiscent of the cry Cehn-Tahr made when in battle, the death cry called the decaliphe. But this one had a more bass pitch.

She couldn't see him in the darkness, but the growl was slowly escalating. She felt hands suddenly grasp her from behind. She felt his teeth on her shoulder, his claws digging into her rib cage. His teeth moved to the back of her neck. She recalled, with growing unease, his comment that if she bent her neck to his teeth he would make her pay for it. Her heart jumped into her throat. He was her commander. She'd known him for three years. But this creature was alien in a way she'd never expected and as threatening as a charging galot.

He felt taller and more massive than he appeared. The growls and the brutal grip of his hands would have been enough to frighten any woman not battle-hardened. She wasn't certain whether or not to fight at this point. He wasn't really hurting her.

While she was considering her options, he suddenly lifted her and literally tossed her across the room.

Gasping at the shock of movement, and the raw strength that had propelled her such a distance, she landed on her back, thankfully on a soft surface. The impact still knocked the breath out of her. Before she could catch it, Dtimun had pinned her, facedown, so that she could not escape. There was a cry, much more like the decaliphe, that chilled her to the bone. Behind her, the growl grew louder. She felt a crushing weight as sharp teeth bit into the back of her neck. To that pain was added, quite suddenly, another pain. Shocking. Humiliating. Infuriating! She clenched her teeth in fury.

"Like…hell…you…do!" she raged at him. Her head whipped around and she caught the muscular forearm beside her and bit it as hard as she could. She tasted blood.

He growled again, and his teeth bit in harder.

She cried out furiously, struggling as the pain increased. She lashed out with one leg and connected with his shin. While he was reacting to that attack, she launched another on his arm with her teeth. He pinned her with ridiculous ease and brought his teeth to her neck again, pushing her down with his formidable weight in a surge of pure aggression.

"How dare you!" she rasped indignantly. All her imagining hadn't prepared her for this sort of domination. When she got her hands free, she was going to pay him back royally!

There was a louder growl, unrelated to her resistance, and then a brief lessening of aggression.

She increased her struggles, sensing weakness, but with all her combat training, she couldn't budge him. She groaned furiously, all her resentments combined in the angry sound. Pain intruded on her anger and she moaned, furious at her own helplessness even as her companion growled again and finally relaxed.

He whipped her onto her back. His fingers locked into hers. In the darkness, she could see only the green glow of his eyes as he looked down at her.

"This is not as I wished it," he said in a voice that sounded odd, different, as if the Standard words were being formed in a throat unaccustomed to making the sounds. "The violence is our shame, the penalty we pay for daring to experiment with our own genetic structure. I would not hurt you for any reason, if the choice were mine. It is not. This is my nature," he ground out. "This violent, animal ferocity."

She was still trying to reconcile her anger with his guilt and find a balance. She had rarely been bested in combat, even by an adversary so superior. She swallowed, hard, and struggled for breath.

His head bent and he brushed his face against hers, tenderly. "Now you can understand why Komak's genetic mix was necessary," he whispered. "Without it, I would have killed you."

There was torment in his deep voice. She realized that he wasn't exaggerating. His claws would have punctured her lungs, as they had on Lagana even when he was in control of himself. His strength was so superior, even with her modifications, that she would have bruises. She recalled hearing him talk about Hahnson's broken back from only the preliminaries of his mating with an exiled Cehn-Tahr woman. Dtimun had said that no method ever discovered by science could lessen the aggression. As she had been three years ago, she could not have survived this.

She was realizing something more, as well. Her mental neutering was supposed to cause excruciating pain if she attempted to mate. It had not. Although, there had been another sort of pain…

"That could not be helped," he said at her ear. His voice was calmer now. "Something a physician should know."

There was almost a teasing note in his voice. She felt herself begin to relax, despite the discomfort. She would never admit that he had frightened her, of course.

"Of course," he murmured drily.

"You stop that," she said firmly. "My thoughts are my own."

He drank in the scent of her. "My father said that my mother attempted to jump out a window at their first mating," he whispered.

That surprised a laugh out of her. "A window?"

"Yes, on the top floor of a very tall building." His tongue brushed her throat as he inhaled the floral scent of her hair. "My father was quick. He caught her as she fell."

His fingers felt odd. Thicker than they appeared. He was incredibly heavy. She also had the impression of massive physical presence, strength, raw power. He seemed much taller, broader, than he appeared. Despite her reengineered bone mass, he was many times her superior in strength. Was the darkness to hide him from her eyes, she wondered, so that she couldn't see what he really looked like?

"An astute guess," he said huskily. His fingers, strong and thick, speared into hers, sliding in between them. "We do not mate as humans do, but as the great galots do. Males dominate by pinning the female at the back of the neck. An undignified, shameful process, which we hide from outworlders. I told you that you might learn things about us which you would not like."

His deep voice was harsh with regret. She began to understand why the Cehn-Tahr were so secretive about their behaviors. Her body slowly began to relax. It wasn't fair to blame him for something that was in-born in him, in all his species. She had agreed to this. It was not against her will. Securing the timeline required sacrifice. Certainly, this episode was as difficult for him as it was for her.

"Yes," he answered the unspoken question somberly. "Intimacy requires a lowering of barriers which is dif-ficult for me. I have always been alone, apart."

"So have I, really," she confessed. She moved and winced. There was a lot of discomfort.

"You must heal the damage, Madeline," he said softly.

"You said the physicians would have to examine me. Couldn't they…?"

His hands contracted. "You misunderstand." His tongue caressed her throat again, producing exquisite sensations. "I have not finished."

Her mind was fuzzy. "But…?"

"Do you think I wish to go through the rest of my life with a memory so brutal and unfeeling as what we just shared?" he asked at her ear. "You will forget. I will not." He stilled. "Heal the damage."

She hesitated, but only for an instant. She was curi-ous about what he meant to do. She used the wrist scan-ner and activated its drug banks. For an instant, when the screen lit to calculate the dosage of nanocells, she got a glimpse of a huge hand with broad fingers which looked nothing like the commander's.

He put his hand over the screen, shielding the light. "You will not look at me," he said firmly. "And you will not touch me, regardless of what happens."

Now she was truly curious. She deactivated the unit. "Why?"

He moved down against her. His tongue rasped against softer flesh, creating sensations that overwhelmed her. She gasped and her fingernails bit into his muscular arms. Involuntarily her hands slid to his back and encountered a long, soft line of fur over his spinal column...

He pulled her hands away and smoothed them over his broad, hair-covered chest. "You will not touch me, except here," he whispered again.

"O...okay," she whispered back. She was barely capable of rational thought, awash on a wave of delight so intense that she shivered.

"Our first encounter did not produce a child," he said huskily. "This one will."

"How can you know...?"

He laughed softly as he felt her shocked reaction. His tongue slid down her throat, over her collarbone. His teeth bit in, gently, and she shivered again.

"This is how we mark our mates," he whispered. "It is a ritual older than time. But I promise you, there will be no pain from it."

She felt thick, soft hair against her skin; more like fur than hair. His mouth opened. She felt his teeth. But at the same moment they bit down, explosive sensations blinded her mind and her body to anything except a wave of pleasure so overwhelming that she gasped and then sobbed helplessly.

"What are you...doing?" she cried out.

He laughed deep in his throat. "Something that you will never learn from falsified black market vids," he whispered.

Her nails bit into his chest. "You wouldn't tell me, and there was no other way to find out," she accused shakily. She groaned and caught her breath. "Dtimun!" she exclaimed.

It was the first time she'd ever used his name. The effect it had on him was explosive. His reaction drew sounds from her that she'd never heard herself make. She hoped the doors were tightly closed.

He heard that thought and chuckled. "The room is soundproof," he whispered.

She cried out, a sound that was almost primeval, piercing and poignant.

He put his mouth over hers and pressed down, hard, a Cehn-Tahr mating custom that they shared with humans. Her cries most likely would not penetrate the walls. But, just in case...

SHE CAME BACK to consciousness very slowly. She was aware of movement. The air stirred around her. A wisp of fabric was draped around her, just before the lights activated.

Dtimun was wearing a red pant-skirt like the one that comprised the Kahn-Bo fighting garment that martial art enthusiasts wore in matches aboard ship. His chest was bare, muscular and covered with thick black hair. He pulled her up so that she was sitting on the edge of the bed and as the fabric dipped, momentarily; his eyes found the unique mark of bonding that he had placed just below her collarbone. The marks reflected ancient hieroglyphs for certain words, whose meanings were an indication of the male's feelings for his mate. There were also other lacerations, deep and painful. Most of them would be on her back. The court physicians should not comment on them; however, the eldest, a female whom Dtimun did not like, might be so bold. He did not want Madeline upset. She was shivering. The vulnerability, even briefly, of such a strong and independent spirit touched him.

His fingers brushed her cheek. "The physicians are waiting. You must be examined. It is the law."

She nodded. Her eyes met his and searched them with silent awe. The experience was beyond anything she'd ever encountered. And now she knew, most certainly, that he was far different than he appeared. He must use a sensor net to disguise his true face, one which would be weakened under emotional stress. Hence, the darkness in the mating chamber.

She knew he saw that thought in her mind, but he ignored it.

He turned away and activated the door. Five female physicians in gray robes, headed by a taller gray-haired one, walked stoically into the room. The gray-haired one stood in front of Madeline and looked at her with blatant distaste. She said something in Cehn-Tahr, in the holy tongue, in a harsh, cold tone.

Dtimun had started to leave, as custom dictated, when he felt the sudden sense of unease, of embarrassment, that rushed into Madeline's mind as the haughty physician looked at her. For the first time in almost three years, he saw her vulnerable, sensitive. It was such a rare reaction for her that all his protective instincts rallied and bristled. He turned, frowning when he saw the way the head physician was studying her. He felt a surge of possession stronger than anything he'd ever experienced in his life, mingled with anger. His jaw tautened and he walked back to stand beside her. He was defying convention, and he did not care. It disturbed him that Madeline was being denigrated by this smug physician. He would not tolerate it in his own house.

The eldest female physician gasped. She made a haughty remark. Dtimun snapped at her in his own tongue. Shocked, she moved back, bowed and abruptly turned to Madeline and reached out, removing the fabric that covered her and dropping it to her waist.

Madeline was puzzled at the physician's behavior. She looked up and saw Dtimun's eyes on her, lingering where his teeth had marked her. But they were appreciative of her soft skin, the delicate form of her body.

The female physician examined the lacerations on Madeline's back with growing distaste. She used her instruments abruptly, without kindness, and then spoke to Dtimun in Cehn-Tahr. Madeline didn't understand the words, but they sounded quite indignant.

He exploded with anger, his tone so cutting, his eyes making such a threat, that the elderly female actually backed away. She lowered her eyes and spoke in a respectful tone, almost toadying.

Dtimun didn't unbend one inch. He gave a curt command. The physician looked shocked, and started to argue. He cut her off and made an imperious gesture toward the door. The female regained her composure, bowed again, paler than when she entered the chamber, and left, very quickly. A younger physician moved forward, bowing to him, smiling gently, and speaking softly. He nodded, obviously still preoccupied and angry.

The young physician treated the wounds on Madeline's back and hips and used a disinfectant only on the scar of bonding. Then she, and the remaining three physicians, bowed, smiling, and started to leave the chamber.

"Could you tell me what that was all about...?" Madeline started to ask the question when she was suddenly sick all over the floor. She fell to her knees, shivering.

"Get Hahnson!" Dtimun called in Cehn-Tahr to the young physician. "Now! Bring him here!"

THE NEXT FEW minutes went by in a blur. Hahnson came running. Dtimun held the fabric around Madeline's nudity and growled furiously at Hahnson when he approached her.

Hahnson stopped in his tracks. A man confronted by a charging galot couldn't have felt more threatened. The alien's posture, barely altered, added to the black of his eyes and the growl would have stopped a decorated combat soldier in his tracks.

"I will not harm you. You must ignore the threat. I cannot help it," Dtimun said tersely, wincing at his own frustrating lack of control even now.

Hahnson smiled. "I know. It's all right. Maddie, can you tell me the symptoms?"

"You can see them...on the floor, Strick," she said with black humor. "I feel so nauseated! My stomach hurts. It's like a knife...!"

"It is the child," Dtimun said huskily. "The growth is immediate, and exponential."

Hahnson grimaced as he looked at the small screen of his wrist unit. "We have to slow the growth. I'm not prepared for this."

"Caneese has a preparation," Madeline said weakly. "She told me about it."

Dtimun called the young physician back into the chamber and rapped out an order. "She will bring it," he told Madeline.

"Can't Caneese…?" she asked, confused.

"Caneese is not allowed to see us," he replied curtly. "It is a breach of protocol."

"Oh." She was confused, but much too sick to argue.

Hahnson injected a drug into the artery at Madeline's neck. "That will help the nausea. But it's only treating symptoms right now. I have no experience with Cehn-Tahr/human babies," he added with a wry smile. "I think this is going to be on-the-job training."

"No doubt," she managed. She was stunned by the notion that she was pregnant. Despite their earlier discussions, even with Komak's assurances, she hadn't really expected it to happen. Her knowledge of pregnancy was limited to a rare assistance at childbirth, but this was far more personal. The physical manifestations were new and startling.

Hahnson looked from one of them to the other. "I don't suppose either of you would like to explain what the hell you think you're doing? I mean, we're talking capital punishment…"

"Chacon is in grave danger. The princess has gone to Benaski Port to warn him," Dtimun told him. "Komak has traveled in time and knows the future. He said that Chacon's death will create a disastrous timeline. Madeline and I must go to Benaski Port in an attempt to save them both, but the masquerade can only work if she carries my child."

"They'll space you both, if you're caught," Hahnson said worriedly.

"That's why you aren't telling anyone, old dear," Madeline told him. "Not even Edris."

Before he could reply, the young physician was back with a cup of what looked like herbal tea. She offered it to Madeline and left the room. Madeline's hands shook as she held the beverage.

"You must drink it all," Dtimun told her, steadying the cup with his own hand. "It will retard the growth of the fetus."

Fetus. The fetus. The baby. She sipped tea and tried to wrap her spinning mind around the fact that she was pregnant. When she and Dtimun had discussed this possibility, she had asked what they would do with a baby. She was a soldier, she had said, she had no place for a child in her life. But now, with the reality of it, she felt a connection with the baby that overwhelmed her. She was carrying a child in her body. She touched her stomach with a sense of awe and fascination. It wasn't, she thought, anything like she'd expected.

Hahnson examined her again, and nodded when he saw the readouts. "You'll do," he told Madeline. "I'll compound some of this for you in Caneese's lab, in a laserdot. She and I will confer on a regimen as well, for your trip." He looked from one stoic, impassive face to the other. "This is very risky."

"We know," Madeline told him. "But the future is at stake."

He sighed. "Then I'll hope for good results." He got up and forced a smile. "Good fortune."

Dtimun locked forearms with him. "In my lifetime,

I have had very few friends. I have always considered you one of them."

"Same here. Take care of each other."

He nodded.

Hahnson left, and Madeline began to feel better. She got her second wind and looked up at Dtimun.

"Sir, do you think you might consider telling me what the devil happened with the physicians?"

His lips made a thin line. "The elder one made a remark I did not like."

"Yes?" she prompted.

"She pointed out that your wounds were in the wrong place. Then she referred to the length of time we spent in the mating chamber."

She cocked her head. She didn't understand.

"Madeline, our mates are subjugated, as female galots are subjugated. The process is brief, and brutal, and it leaves wounds on the chest and abdomen, not on the back. Also it is a breach of protocol to enjoy it."

"It is?" she asked, and mischief suddenly sparkled in her green eyes.

He glared at her expression. "You will never speak of this," he said abruptly.

"Would I do that, sir?" she murmured innocently. "As you know, I always obey your every order."

"You never listen to an order unless it suits you," he correctly curtly. "But if you ignore this one, you will pay for it."

She gave him a wry look. "I'm not in the habit of discussing intimate things," she replied. "Besides, people may speculate, but no one will ever know what happened in here, anyway."

He lifted an eyebrow haughtily. All at once his own

eyes went green with amusement. "For which we are obliged to the architect who soundproofed the chamber," he said with the straightest face she'd ever seen.

He had rarely seen her speechless. It was amusing. Her face was almost as red as her hair. She averted her eyes with obvious embarrassment.

"You fought me," he mused.

She cleared her throat. "Sorry," she said, thinking it was probably another breach of protocol.

"You need not apologize," he chuckled. "I quite enjoyed it, once the shock wore off." He knelt beside her and touched her long, damp hair. His eyes met hers. They gleamed like pure gold. It was a color she'd only seen in them once before. "I do not like submission," he said in a husky, deep voice. His hand gripped her hair, hard, and pulled her face under his so that he could see directly into her eyes. He looked down his long, aristocratic nose at her with blatant possession. Her breath caught. The sensations the action aroused were new and shocking.

"That's a good thing," she said unsteadily, "because you'll never get it from me."

He smiled. He rubbed his head against hers in an oddly feline way, making a caress of it. His hand relaxed and speared through her long hair, savoring its softness. "We mated only to produce a child, to enhance a covert mission…or so it began." His hand contracted again and he growled softly as the contact with the soft skin at her nape produced delicious sensations. She felt them, too. "It is strange, to find such compatibility between two such different species."

She touched his chiseled mouth with her fingertips.

She lowered her eyes to his bare chest. She fought a laugh. "The physicians seemed quite shocked."

He laughed, deep in his throat, and rubbed his cheek against hers affectionately. "So was I. I have never taken so much pleasure from a female," he said bluntly. His hands pulled her gently to him and enfolded her. "I deeply regret the violence at the beginning. But I did tell you once, did I not, that passion is always violent."

She slid her arms around his neck and held on tight, closing her eyes. "You did, but I didn't understand what you meant until now. Despite those—" she pulled back and stared at him suspiciously "—those dreams I had, that you said you weren't responsible for."

"I lied. The discomfort began to affect my ability to think rationally." His hands smoothed her shoulders gently. "The 'dreams' are one of several coping strategies we employ in order to survive the long abstinences," he told her. "Each time we mate, a child is created. One is dangerous. Two at once is a death sentence, even for a Cehn-Tahr woman."

He was explaining something, very discreetly. "You mate only to have children?"

"The customs and culture of our society dictate that," he agreed.

She cocked her head and her eyes twinkled. "Dictate it. But do people really abstain between children?" she asked. "Komak said they didn't."

"Since we do not discuss such intimate behaviors openly, the question is not easily answered."

That brought to mind something that had piqued her curiosity before. She sketched his face with soft eyes. "Those holovid generators at Kolmankash," she murmured. "Are they really used for vid games?"

He smoothed back her damp hair affectionately. "When we are separated from our mates," he said, "they permit an intimacy which is almost indistinguishable from reality," he said after a minute. He looked at her sternly. "This is another thing you will never share with an outworlder."

She saluted him.

He glared at her.

She laughed. "We agreed a long time ago that I'm discreet," she reminded him. "I never tell anything I know."

He sighed. "No. You never do." He looked down at her body in its thin covering. "How does it feel?" he asked suddenly.

"Feel?" she repeated curiously.

"My child lies in your womb," he said slowly, as if the idea, the concept, was a source of awe. His eyes, softly gold, met hers. "How does it feel?"

Her lips parted. She searched his eyes. "I don't have the words," she faltered. She touched his face and all the intensity of her feelings for him made her radiant, as if she were glowing inside with some secret heat. "You'll have to find them, in my mind."

Her awe and delight were there, along with her feelings for him, so intense that he almost felt the impact physically.

He seemed fascinated with her. And not just with her. His gaze dropped to her stomach. He reached down and touched it with just his fingertips, and caught his breath.

She frowned. He looked shocked.

As he was. The Dacerian woman had told him, decades past, that she carried his child. And now he knew that it was a lie. He knew it, because he felt his child, communicated with his child at some molecular level, sensed the child in every cell of his body. His teeth clenched as he relived the anguish just after her death. He had blamed his father. Now, horribly, he was forced to face his own error. If she had lied about one thing, it was certain that she had lied about others.

He recalled the Dacerian's easy acceptance of him when they mated, her bland submission. It was different with Madeline. Madeline had fought him. But then, she had become as fiercely responsive as she had been fiercely resistant. Madeline loved him. The Dacerian woman…never had. And he only now realized it.

She felt the indecision and sorrow. She smoothed her hand gently over his black hair. "You can feel the child," she whispered, surprised that she knew that so certainly.

He opened his eyes and looked into hers. Sensation overwhelmed him. He felt comfort, sympathy, joy in her touch. "Yes," he said after a minute, and he smiled gently. "I can feel our child."

She leaned forward and touched her forehead to his. It was a moment out of time, when she wished the clock would never move again. She wanted it to last forever.

There was a faint noise at the door, like scratching. He lifted his head and stared into Madeline's soft eyes for another few seconds. His were still that incredible shade of gold. She didn't know what it meant. But before she could ask him, he stood up, suddenly remote and stoic, as if they were in his office together discussing strategy. The intimacy fell away at once.

He turned. The door opened and a tall, somber woman with her black hair in a bun approached them. She bowed.

Madeline looked at her with curiosity. She smiled shyly. The smile was returned.

"Sfilla," the woman told her. She pointed to herself. "Sfilla."

"Madeline," came the gentle reply.

Dtimun turned to her. "Sfilla will be your companion on our journey. She will act as cook and personal aide, as well. She has been with my family for many years, and is one of its most trusted members. You will go with her now to your own quarters."

"Yes, sir," Madeline acknowledged.

Sfilla looked at her with astonishment. "You call him 'sir'?" she exclaimed, and worked hard at pronouncing the unfamiliar Standard. Still, there was hardly a trace of an accent.

Madeline blinked. "I've been calling him 'sir' for almost three years," she explained and smiled as she looked at him. "Habits are hard to break, even under the circumstances." She shrugged. "Hey, at least I'm not saluting you," she said in her defense.

His eyes narrowed thoughtfully. "Do that at Benaski Port and I will lock you in a bath cubicle and lose the key," he threatened.

In defiance, she stood at attention. "Notice I'm not saluting," she said with irrepressible humor.

Sfilla giggled. Dtimun sighed. "It is a complicated situation," he told the woman, with a wry smile.

"As you say," Sfilla replied.

"Are all those people still out there?" Madeline asked suddenly, bringing Dtimun's amused eyes back to her.

She was tugging at the flimsy fabric and looking decidedly uncomfortable.

"They have been told that the mating was productive," he told her. "They have retired to the great room, where they will consume beverages and food for another little space of time, and then they will go home."

"They won't... I mean, they can be trusted?" she worried.

"Even if they could not, Caneese can be quite intimidating," he chuckled. "I assure you, no word of this will reach the Dectat, if that is what concerns you."

She nodded.

His eyes swept over her and narrowed with pure possession. She was more beautiful now than he had ever seen her. And she was his now. She belonged to him. She would never be able to mate with a human. It gave him a sense of utter delight to know that.

She didn't understand the look in his eyes, one she'd never seen in them, and he didn't answer her curiosity. He turned away and abruptly left the room.

Chuckling, Sfilla went to fetch a robe out of what passed for a closet and helped drape her in it.

"You must not be embarrassed," Sfilla said softly when she noted the discomfort in Madeline's expression. "It is part of life. And you have a child from it. A noble result. A son!"

Madeline hadn't thought to use her wrist scanner. She touched the slight, hard mound with wonder. "A son." The word sounded as if it held magic.

Sfilla laughed. "You have been a soldier for many years. Now you must become a Cehn-Tahr aristocrat's consort, so that you are not identified at Benaski Port as the soldier that you are. That will be my chore, to tutor you."

Madeline raised an eyebrow. "Oh?"

Sfilla pursed her lips. "And perhaps you can teach

me the art of hand-to-hand combat," she said, smiling at some private joke.

Madeline grinned. "Deal!"

LATER, AFTER SHE had bathed and a small meal had been brought to her, she sat in the sunlight filtering through her window and tried to make sense of what had happened. Everyone said that the mating was brutal and barbaric, that Cehn-Tahr women sometimes would forsake bonding because they were so frightened of it. Madeline had not found it barbaric at all, except just at first. She wondered what other females had found so terrifying.

"Passion," Dtimun replied to her silent question.

Her head turned, her expression questioning. He was dressed in robes, as he had been when they attended the Altair reception. He looked elegant.

She smiled. "You said once that I would have nightmares."

He chuckled. "I underestimated you. In many ways."

"Sir?"

He groaned. "Madeline, you must stop referring to me as 'sir.' It will arouse suspicion."

"Sorry." She peered up at him. "I really have to stop saluting you, too?"

He glared at her.

"Okay, I'll try. I promise." She cocked her head. "I thought I might have sprains or broken limbs from the way everybody talked about it," she said. "It wasn't brutal. Not as I define brutality."

He moved closer. "Cehn-Tahr women dislike physical boldness. A predator attacks weakness."

She began to understand. His aggression had diminished when she fought him.

"Exactly," he replied. He perched on the edge of the bay window that overlooked the formal garden. His eyes were a soft golden color as they searched hers. "You were not afraid of me." He pursed his lips and reconsidered. "Well, perhaps a little, at the beginning."

"I knew you wouldn't hurt me deliberately," she said simply. She glared at him. "Although…"

"It was unavoidable." He chuckled softly. "And you were not without defenses," he added wryly, and held up a forearm with tooth marks to show her.

"Sorry," she said with a grin. "It was unavoidable."

He smiled. "You bit me as a child when I helped your father rescue you from terrorists," he reminded her. "I prefer spirit to acquiescence."

"Fortunately for you, I'm never acquiescent," she said.

He searched her eyes. It was only beginning to occur to him how large a place she occupied in his thoughts, in his life. "You know me as few people ever have," he said after a minute. "I find it difficult to relate to most outworlders."

"I know how you feel. I don't get along well with most humans," she agreed. "I'm very fond of Strick and Holt, but even so, I could never talk to them about things I could say to you."

That made him feel warm inside. He didn't like her closeness to the other males, but he didn't remark on it.

"Would you have attacked Flannegan, that day in the gym?" she asked abruptly, alluding to an incident that had almost betrayed his need of her to the military authorities, before her nearly fatal crash on Akaashe.

It would have cost him his life, if his government had found out.

"I would have killed him," he said bluntly. "Possessive behavior is part of the mating ritual. Even now, Stern and Hahnson are not safe if they come near you." He laughed shortly. "I had to fight my instincts to permit Hahnson to treat you. It was difficult." His eyes narrowed. "I do not want another male to touch you."

She pursed her lips. "I'm glad to hear it, because I would go ballistic if any other female touched you," she confessed firmly.

Her possessiveness of him was a delight. He smiled. "Jealousy. It is an odd concept. I have never felt it until now."

"It's just the mating ritual," she assured him. "When we save Chacon and the princess and the child is gone, and my memory is wiped, you won't feel it anymore." She didn't look at him as she said it. The removal of the child was something that hurt her even to think about. Amazing, since regressing it had been her own solution to the aftermath of their covert mission.

She felt a tremor in her stomach and put her hand on it with mingled delight and scientific curiosity. The cell division progressed at an exponential rate. Cehn-Tahr babies, she'd learned from researching in the fortress's extensive library, grew at a vastly accelerated rate. Odd, that there were no pictorial depictions of them in any of the literature, she thought idly. She could not know that Dtimun had ordered the images concealed when he learned of her research efforts.

"Anything you require will be provided," he told her. "And Hahnson will be nearby until our departure. I had

Mallory sent to the capitol on a pretext so that she will not know of the pregnancy."

She nodded. She drew in a long breath. The child was growing quite rapidly, despite the herbs that were meant to retard the growth, and it was painful. She had nausea as well, that became debilitating from time to time. She had to carefully monitor her health. The disparity in sizes between human and Cehn-Tahr was going to be a real problem if the mission lasted longer than expected. "When do we leave for Benaski Port?"

"In a few days," he said. "The child must be visible when we arrive there."

She looked up, frowning. "Why couldn't I have pretended to be pregnant?"

"It would have been discovered. Cehn-Tahr are not the only telepaths in the three galaxies," he said, surprising her. "The deception, once uncovered, would destroy any chance of saving Chacon and Lyceria."

"I see."

He was looking at her intently. She lifted her eyes to his and found turbulence in them. "Why are you looking at me that way?" she asked.

He reached down and touched her hair, smoothing it with his fingers. "What we imagine the future to be is usually quite different from the reality. In another place, another time, many things might have been possible that are not, now," he said quietly. He stopped, letting the thought trail away, as his voice did.

She was confused by the feelings he aroused when he looked at her. She shifted in the chair. Her eyes met his again, and were puzzled once more by their burnished gold shade. It was one she'd never seen before.

"It is a color which is not shown to anyone outside

the family," he explained patiently. "That is why you have not seen it."

"Oh." She laughed, then frowned. "But I have. Your eyes were that color when you rescued me, on Akaashe," she added, puzzled.

"A result of the mating behavior," he lied. It had been more than that, but he didn't want to think about it just yet. He traced her cheek, his gaze still intent on her face. "So many differences," he mused. "But in many more ways, we are alike. We must concentrate on the similarities during our time in Benaski Port, so that we do not arouse suspicion."

"I don't suppose you'll arm me for the mission?" she murmured mischievously.

He lifted an eyebrow. "Only under threat of immediate attack by squadrons of Rojoks."

She sighed. "I might have known."

"You will not require a weapon. I will protect you and the child," he said.

Odd, the feeling those words provoked, in a very capable and independent spirit. They made her feel warm inside, in a way she never had before.

It made him feel the same. It was disturbing. He turned away. "I have duties to attend to. If you need anything, you have only to call. A servant will answer."

"Servants, luxurious clothing, every whim attended to," she said. "It's difficult to adjust."

He smiled. "Despite how it may seem, my own life has been quite regimented and sparse in the way of luxuries. It is a change for me, too, this new lifestyle."

Her gaze slid over his handsome face. "It's only temporary."

He nodded. His eyes went to her belly, where his

child was growing. His face hardened and he turned
away. It wouldn't do to get too involved with her pregnancy.

She watched him go with sad eyes. She touched her
stomach with wonder. She hadn't really believed it was
possible. She was amazed at how much she wanted
the child. That possibility hadn't even occurred to her.
She turned back to the balcony. It would be unwise to
dwell on impossible things. She looked up as a small,
personal transport flew over and sighed. It was going
to be a long few days.

CHAPTER FOUR

MADELINE THOUGHT SHE knew the commander of the Holconcom quite well after serving aboard his vessel for almost three years. But, the private person was far removed from the military leader.

Despite the somewhat disturbing physical events of the recent past, she was still comfortable with him when they were alone. He walked with her in the gardens of the fortress, pointing out the various forms of flora and even quoting the names in High Cehn-Tahr, the ancient language, the holy tongue.

"That dialect is familiar," she said. "I've heard it spoken by the *kehmatemer*. But it isn't in current use widely, is it?"

"No," he agreed. "The emperor insisted on keeping the ancient language alive, so that the roots of our people would endure. He considers that language is the basis of culture."

"I see. So the Dectat uses it in discussions, and the *kehmatemer* use it among themselves, since they protect the officials of the Dectat."

He smiled. "Exactly."

She closed her eyes and drank in the exquisite fragrance of the *canolithe*, which grew in the nearby woods. "I smelled canolithe for the first time in a library on Altair 6 where we were on maneuvers," she recalled with a smile. "It had been recorded in the sensor logs and reproduced by an olfactory process known only to the Altairians."

He turned and looked down at her with quiet appreciation of her beauty, enhanced by the child she was carrying. His child. He felt possession wash over him like a wave. He had never felt it like this, certainly not for the Dacerian woman long ago whom, he was only beginning to realize, had an agenda that he had never perceived.

She became aware of his scrutiny and looked up. "Is something wrong?"

He shook his head. "I was remembering the day I brought you here, when I showed the *canolithe* to you," he said with a gentle smile.

Her green eyes brightened. "It was the happiest day of my life." She hadn't meant to say it aloud. She flushed a little self-consciously and averted her eyes. "I mean, the military doesn't get much opportunity to walk around in places like this."

He stopped, deep in thought. "At the time, the differences between our species seemed insurmountable," he said quietly. He turned and looked down at her. There was turmoil in the warping colors of his eyes. "There are things you can never know about us," he added.

She frowned. "What sort of things?"

He sighed. His hand went out to touch her long, reddish-gold hair, given a radiant halo in the light from the two suns of Memcache. "Other dissimilarities that are not apparent. And political considerations that are even more forbidding than the physical differences."

"You mean, because you're an aristocrat and I'm a

common soldier," she said, and didn't take offense. "I know…"

"That is not what I mean," he interrupted. "Madeline, our emperor was a common soldier, too. He came from an agricultural background. His people worked the soil for generations. When he was young, he became infatuated with the daughter of the house for which his family worked."

"Oh, dear," she said, anticipating how that would have played out.

He laughed. "You assume correctly. Her people were outraged that he would expect to have her. But they underestimated his ambition. He organized a group of soldiers who were outcast from the military because they were clones of their originals, who had been killed in action."

She gasped.

"Yes," he said. "My people were once as intolerant of clones as yours are now. The emperor looked not at their construction, but at the way they fought, and their loyalty to him. He coaxed the best scientists of our culture to work for him, to concern themselves with genetic engineering that would make his soldiers the superior of any they might meet in combat. He also focused their efforts on the development of microcyborg technology, to accentuate their strengths."

"That's how his imperial bodyguard, his Praetorians, was formed," she guessed.

He laughed. "This is how the Holconcom was formed," he corrected.

Her lips fell apart with surprise.

"Once the improvements were made, he had the *Mor-*

cai built to his own specifications and made it the Holconcom flagship."

She frowned. "Those innovations must have required genius. But you said he was from an agricultural background."

"He was an eternal student," he said, glancing around him at the natural beauty of the setting. "He never stopped reading, studying. He won a place in our university system through his own efforts rather than any Clan connections and graduated first in his class with doctorates in physics and chemistry and emerillium technology."

"Heavens! I've never read any of that in textdiscs!"

"It is not common knowledge. But the female with whom he wished to bond came from ancient royalty. His wisdom, his accomplishments, meant nothing to her family."

"Snobs," she muttered.

He chuckled. "In that sense, yes, they were."

"But he did win her, in the end?"

"Of course. He never relinquished a goal. He determined to have her, no matter what the cost. So he took the Holconcom on a decades-long mission of conquest. When he was done, he had conquered a hundred and fifty worlds. The confederation has dwindled somewhat in the past two decades, with the advent of the sovereignty programs in the three galaxies, but we still claim more than a hundred colonies. The emperor set up committees to govern and improve living conditions within the colonies and sent experts in all fields out to work with their own leaders. His innovations were so extraordinary that the conquered governments never sought liberation, in those days. They were lifted out of isolation and poverty into wealth, given sovereignty, and encouraged to send representation to the Dectat to discuss policies that would affect them." He glanced at her as they began walking again, smiling. "He became emperor through acclamation with not one single dissenting vote. At that point, I might add, the female's family was offering their daughter to him."

"I imagine they expected high positions at court in return," she mused.

"If that was the case, they were disappointed. He had them moved to a distant province, where they still live. They have never been permitted at court." He chuckled. "He has a long memory and he does not forgive easily. His pride was severely damaged by their attitude toward him when he had nothing except his brilliance and ambition to offer."

"I don't blame him," she said. "But it must have been hard on his consort."

"Not at all. Her family had long treated her as an outcast because she obtained degrees in—" He stopped abruptly. "Let us say that they did not approve of her goal of higher education. They had also attempted to bond her with a much older citizen of great wealth and position."

"Attempted?"

He laughed. "Her father invited him to the house and arranged a bonding ceremony. They only told her when the official arrived to perform the bonding. She left the room, climbed out a window, down a tree beside her suite of rooms and hid out in the forest for two days until the older citizen left. When she returned, she informed her father that the next time he attempted such a union, she would jump from the tree rather than climb down it. He was proud of his position in society. It would be a scandal for the only daughter of the house to commit suicide. She prevailed. And, later, she became Empress of all the Cehn-Tahr."

She laughed, too. "What a lady," she said with admiration. "That's not the sort of person I thought an empress would be."

"Her exploits were legend when she was young."

She frowned. "Didn't she leave the emperor?"

"Yes. There was a tragedy which separated them."

He didn't elaborate and she was hesitant to pursue the subject. It seemed to make him uncomfortable. She drew in a long breath and sighed. "The *canolithe* are exquisite," she said.

"Yes, I have always thought so…"

He stopped abruptly as a huge galot suddenly appeared out of nowhere in the garden just ahead of them. The feline's sleek black coat glittered like diamonds in the sunlight. It had large green eyes and its mouth, slightly open, displayed snowy-white fangs. Its paws were enormous, and although the claws were retracted, she knew they could appear like lightning if it attacked. The species had a reputation for being aggressive and merciless.

Her hand went protectively to her belly. She wasn't afraid for herself. But the thought of what those claws could do to the child alarmed her.

"Be still," Dtimun said quietly.

"No, I thought I'd sprint across the yard to the house," she said in a tone dripping sarcasm, "and try to outrun him!"

There was a muffled sound from the galot.

"Why are you here?" Dtimun asked the cat, while

Madeline stared at him as if he'd gone mad, speaking to an animal.

"I wanted to see the female who carries your cub," the cat spoke, in a voice that was reminiscent of a cat hissing, except the sounds were intelligible as words. Madeline was surprised. She had no idea that the galot species had speech at all, despite zoological studies which suggested it due to the structure of its throat.

"You chased the small Nagaashe child and frightened it," Dtimun said curtly. "You were banished."

"Only for a time," the cat said, and made what sounded like a chuckle. "You should know, *Dakaashe*, that you cannot banish me for long."

Dakaashe. Madeline had never heard the word. She wondered what it meant.

"If Rognan sees you, there will be a war," Dtimun mused.

"He is eating fruit. It is the time when he naps." He moved forward toward Madeline, very slowly, stalking her.

Dtimun gave a low, warning growl. The cat ignored him.

Madeline stood her ground, examining him with curious fascination. He was all muscle. And as he drew closer, she realized that he was at least three times the size of a Terravegan tiger. If he stood on his hind legs, he would be taller than Dtimun.

He stopped a foot away from her and looked into her eyes. He was almost level with them. "You are Ruszel."

She caught her breath and laughed. "Yes!"

"The galots know of you," he said. "You called Meg-Ravens to save the Nagaashe child from me."

She bit her lower lip. "I'm fond of the Nagaashe," she began defensively.

The big cat laughed. "It was a novel solution," he replied in his odd speech. "I am not angry. I would not have harmed the Nagaashe child. They share tech with us, so they are our allies. I simply like to play."

"Too much, at times," Dtimun said curtly, relaxing his taut posture. Had the big cat threatened Madeline or his child, he would have attacked without hesitation, despite the fact that their four-legged visitor was familiar to him.

The big cat turned to him. "You cannot play. You have forgotten how."

"Have I?"

It was one of the more surprising moments of Madeline's life, what happened next. Her dignified commanding officer ran toward the cat at top speed, pounced on him and then rolled on the ground, cuffing at him. It was like watching two cats play. They chased each other around the garden, becoming blurs as they revealed the speeds they were capable of. No terrestrial cat could have outrun them. It was like on Lagana, when Dtimun had attacked the Rojok officer who threatened Madeline, that same incredible speed that made him almost a blur. Apparently galots were capable of it, too.

They went up trees and down them, over rocks, through the small, clear stream that ran around the property. Finally, exhausted and winded, they stopped beside Madeline.

The commander's hair was mussed from the play and he was laughing. Really laughing. Madeline found him fascinating like that.

He noted her curiosity. "This is Kanthor," he said,

introducing his prone, panting companion. "We played together when I could barely walk. He lives on Mem-cache from time to time, although his true home is on a planet in the Eridanus system."

Madeline smiled at him. "Where researchers try to learn about your culture," she mused.

"Yes," Kanthor replied as he panted. "We enjoy their visits. They are quite tasty."

It took her a minute to get that, and she burst out laughing.

"He is not making a joke," Dtimun said, and he was unusually watchful.

"I know." Her eyes twinkled. "Sir, on ancient earth there was a race of cats called Tigers. They were notorious for being man-eaters. I'm not shocked, you know. Felines are simply doing what their nature dictates."

"Yes. It is a feline trait, to eat live prey," he said in an expressionless tone.

"Not only felines," she replied with a sigh. "Humans, too, I'm afraid."

He stared at her, shocked.

She flushed. "Sorry, I shouldn't have said that, I guess."

He moved closer. "Explain. Please," he added when she was hesitant.

She grimaced. "Well, you see, in terrible wars in our history, rations ran out on battlefields. There was nothing to feed prisoners of war. When they were desperate enough, they ate each other. It isn't something we're proud of, you understand, but it's part of our culture. Not that we share that knowledge with other species…!"

He had lifted her from the ground, embraced her almost hungrily.

She didn't know what to think. Her arms slid around his neck and she embraced him as well, until his fury abated and he was gentle.

"Forgive me," he said roughly, drawing back.

She stared up at him with wide, unblinking green eyes. "I thought you would be repulsed, to know something so…distasteful…about my species," she said hesitantly.

"That is because there are secrets you still do not know about mine," he replied tersely.

She wasn't slow. She smiled. "Those stories they tell about the Cehn-Tahr in battle, devouring their prey. They aren't just stories, are they?"

He hesitated, but only for a moment. She had been honest. He could be the same.

"No, Madeline," he replied. "They are not just stories. It was a means of survival at first, and then a way to maintain the fear our enemies felt for us."

"It is quite effective," Kanthor mused, and made a facsimile of laughter, deep in his throat. "It keeps researchers from pestering us."

Madeline chuckled. "We noticed."

"She has no fear of us," Kanthor told Dtimun. "She is worthy to carry your cub."

Madeline's hand went to the mound under her robes. As she recalled the fate of the child inside her, a sweeping sorrow darkened her mind.

Cehn-Tahr and the cat stared at her intently.

"Don't tell me," she thought to Kanthor. "You can read minds, too."

"Of course," the cat replied silently. "Where do you think the Cehn-Tahr acquired the ability, if not from our genetic material?"

Kanthor got to his feet, all four of them, and padded back to Madeline. "I may not reveal all that I know," he told her with a glance at Dtimun, who was scowling at him. "But you should not be so concerned with possibilities, especially those which may not occur."

She smiled at him. "I try not to dwell on them."

"I would have liked a cub of my own," Kanthor said surprisingly. "But my mate died of a fever. I have never wanted another. She was, like you, unique."

Madeline was touched. She reached out a hand to stroke his mane and immediately withdrew it, for fear of offending.

He chuckled. "You may stroke me, if you like. I learned to tolerate it many years ago, from him." He indicated the commander, who chuckled. "The Cehn-Tahr are still very humanoid in some respects."

Madeline touched the thick, soft fur, and smiled. "On my peoples' homeworld, Earth, there were ferocious cats only a little smaller than you. There was a word that would apply quite well to touching them this way: suicide."

"So it is the lure of the forbidden," Kanthor chuckled.

"You could put it that way, I suppose." She withdrew her hand. "It was an honor. Thank you."

His eyebrows lifted. He looked at Dtimun with affection. "Yes," he said. "She is worthy of you. And the cub." He growled. "You should not permit tradition to exact such a price from you."

Dtimun's chin lifted. "I have been thinking this."

"Would anyone care to explain what you're talking about?" Madeline asked.

They both looked at her. They didn't speak.

She threw up her hands.

"We will meet again," Kanthor told Madeline.

She smiled. "I'll look forward to...to..." She looked around, aghast. He was gone. She stared at the commander. "How did he do that?"

He moved to her and smiled. He didn't answer the question.

She recalled that the Nagaashe could jump through time and space and that Kanthor had said the Nagaashe shared tech with his species. She had questions, but she saved them for another time. "I would never mention it to any researcher, but I can understand now why they risk their lives trying to learn about the galots. They're absolutely incredible."

He studied her with affection. "Yes." He looked around at the high platform, carved from the rock, where he often found Madeline sitting. "This is not your first sight of the rock. I have seen you here, sitting," he said. "How did you find this place?"

"Wandering around," she said. "I like walking. It helps with the pain." She studied him through narrowed eyes. "I can't read your mind, exactly, but I get impressions, emotions. This place makes you sad."

He sighed. "My elder brother and I played war here, as boys. Our father supplied us with holographic projectors, so that we could build armies and fight, learn to command. We spent many happy hours here."

"Something happened to him. Something tragic."

He nodded. He leaned against the smooth face of the rock, reminiscent of terrestrial marble, and stared toward the distant mountains. "He did not like the policies of the emperor, what he thought of as the enslavement of other species. He was also violently opposed to the genetic manipulation. He refused to let his son be a subject of such manipulation, which put him in conflict with the emperor. He joined a renegade political organization and paired with an Altair commando group, to effect the rescue of a colony of Cehn-Tahr who were scheduled for genetic manipulation." His eyes grew turbulent with colors. "I was sent, as the new commander of the Holconcom, to stop him."

She grimaced.

He glanced at her and felt the empathy in her thoughts. "I tried to reason with him, but his mind was full of plans to kill the emperor. He had already employed assassins in that endeavor. He thought that it was the only way to stop the genetic manipulation." He paused. "My brother's fate would have been a public execution," he said tersely. "He would have been shamed, humiliated, and his family along with him. Clan is everything to us. We live and die to spare it dishonor."

She recalled that the commander never referred to his own Clan, ever.

He read the thought, but didn't reply to it. He was still lost in memory. "He knew what his fate would be. He told me that he would spare my mother and younger brother and sister, and me, the pain of his shame. Without warning, he attacked the Holconcom, with his ragtag followers." He drew in a sharp breath. "It was over in seconds. You know from serving with us that if we are attacked, for any reason, we retaliate immediately and mercilessly, as a unit." He averted his face. "I killed my brother. The emperor knew that I would have to, but he sent me, anyway. That is one reason we have not spoken for decades." He didn't mention the other reason. His jaw tautened. "Your Tri-Galaxy Council offered me a medal for it," he said harshly. "The Legion of Merit. I threw it in Lokar's face and walked out of the council chambers. It was a long time before I spoke to him again."

She moved in front of him and looked up. "I'm sorry. I don't know what it would be like to have siblings," she said quietly. "I mean, I might have them, there might be others like me grown from the same basic biological material. But I wouldn't be allowed to know." She smiled sadly. "My society doesn't tolerate familial ties, as you already know. My father broke rules to maintain contact with me. He risked his life, in fact."

He touched her cheek gently and smiled. "Caneese is fond of him."

"Excuse me?"

"He came home with me when he was wounded, during the last days of the Great Galaxy War, shortly after we rescued you and some other Terravegan children from terrorists," he recalled. "He and Caneese had a conversation to which I was not allowed access." He frowned. "But I believe it had something to do with the reason you chose medicine as a career alternative while you were in the Amazon Division."

She was surprised. "It was my choice…"

He chuckled. "Caneese can, shall we say, influence choices." He frowned. "Strange, I had never considered her part in all this."

"That prophecy," she said slowly.

He nodded. "Exactly."

She wrapped her arms around herself. "It's rather unnerving. Prophecies, I mean."

"Especially when they seem to be valid." He drew her against him and enveloped her with his arms. "You are chilled."

"Just a little."

He laid his cheek against her hair and closed his eyes. She had surprised him, both with her acceptance of Kanthor and her revelation of unsavory human traits. For the first time, he felt a whisper of hope for the future. Perhaps Kanthor was right, and political considerations were less important than he supposed. He could continue in the military, if it came down to that choice.

"Since you're being forthright about hidden issues, can you tell me why you hate physicians so much?" she asked.

He laughed. "I do not hate you."

"Not me. Your own physicians."

He hesitated. "There was an incident, long ago, with a faction of humans. It was a tragedy, provoked by them but perpetrated by ourselves. I ordered our medics to attend to the survivors, and they refused. They said that it would foul their instruments to use them on an inferior species."

She drew back and looked up at him. "You have court physicians who would never make such a statement. I've known other Cehn-Tahr medics with the same devotion to duty, who would treat anyone, regardless of race or species."

"Yes, I have been intolerant," he agreed. He smiled at her. "Perhaps all it needed was the influence of a fire-haired human physician to remove my prejudices."

She grinned. "Exactly!"

He bent and rubbed his face against hers with gentle affection. She closed her eyes, aware of an odd sensation where his hair was, as if he had a mane there. She laughed, although she thought she perceived a faint stiffening in his posture as she processed and then dismissed the stray thought.

"I have never heard you laugh as much as you have, since we have been here," he commented after a minute.

"I could say the same thing." She pulled back and looked up at him with a grin. "My dignified commanding officer, romping with a galot."

He chuckled. "We play like cats. Quite often, among ourselves." His eyes twinkled with mischief. "And, at times, even with outworlders."

As he spoke, he lifted her in his arms and ran like the wind, prompting a wild laugh from her as she clung to him to avoid being dropped. He went up and down rocks, over fallen tree trunks, over hills and valleys. Finally he stopped, just at the foot of the steps that led up to the fortress and looked down into her flushed, radiant, laughing face.

He felt a jolt of emotion as he stared at her with tenderness. These emotions were new and disturbing. They were completely unlike those he had felt, so long ago, for the Dacerian woman.

He realized that it would tear his soul to give up his mate, to say nothing of the child she carried. It had been a shadowy concept when they discussed the mission to save Chacon. Now it was something else.

Her smile faded as she perceived his unease. "What is it?" she asked.

He drew in a long breath. "It is not as I expected, this bonding."

She cocked her head and stared at him. "It isn't?"

His eyes burned gold as they met hers. His arms tightened just perceptibly. "It will be…difficult—" he chose the word carefully, and bit it off, as if it were distasteful "—to return to the life we knew."

Sadness washed over her. "Yes," she said quietly. "At least, I won't remember any of it. But Strick said that it would be impossible to wipe your memory."

"That is true." His eyes narrowed. "And you might not realize it, but you will retain vestiges of memory that will disturb your thoughts from time to time, like shadows that are seen, but not clearly."

She nodded. "That isn't common knowledge."

He put her back on her feet. "It was necessary to use the memory wipe on Caneese, just after she lost her eldest son," he said quietly. "Only in a limited way, and only to dull the impact of the grief. She became suicidal."

She grimaced. "I'm so sorry," she said. "I didn't know…!"

"She does not speak of it. The wipe was unsuccessful, although it had the advantage of smoothing the more difficult aspects of the tragedy. Since, there have been other tragedies in her life."

"No wonder she lives among religious people."

He nodded. "She says that it is the only peace she has known in decades." His expression became less somber, and his eyes flashed green. "The old fellow has been in contact with her. That is a new, and surprising development, since they have not spoken for many years."

"Really?" she exclaimed, smiling.

"I think they may meet, at some point," he added. "That is because of you. The old fellow was rigid in his beliefs and his prejudices. None of us could approach him, even if we had been amenable to it."

"He seemed quite formal when I first met him on

Ondar," she agreed. "And hostile, as well." She frowned. "He had some very odd ideas about what human females were like." She pursed her lips and her green eyes twinkled. "Women in short skirts running and screaming from terrifying 'space monsters,'" she added with mock fear. "Did you think we were like that, too, when you first encountered us?"

He chuckled. "Not after I saw you fight during our escape from the Rojok prison camp at Ahkmau," he told her. "But he was familiar with the old Terran vids, and he thought human females were docile and fearful of violence of any sort. What a shock it must have been for him when you attacked the Rojok and saved his life."

"He wasn't too thrilled about it, at first," she recalled. "But when he learned that I wrecked bars protecting the reputation of my CO, his attitude changed abruptly," she laughed.

His eyebrows arched.

She told him about the conversation she had with the old fellow.

He chuckled. "It amuses me that he unbent long enough to speak to you at all," he said. "His contempt for humans was far-reaching just after the Great Galaxy War."

"Why?"

"His…" He stopped. "My brother," he corrected, "had as his advisor a human general," he said curtly. "My brother was gullible and the human had nothing but contempt for the Cehn-Tahr government. The old fellow hated him, and because of him, all humans." His lips pursed. "At least, until you saved his life."

She had some serious suspicions about the commander's relationship to the old fellow, but she kept them to herself, and disguised them with mathematics.

He cocked his head. "You are attempting to hide things from me again," he mused.

"Just little things of no importance whatsoever," she said, smiling. "When do we leave for Benaski Port?" she added seriously. She indicated her belly. "Even a blind man could see that I'm pregnant now."

"You and I and Sfilla will leave tomorrow," he said. He drew her to him and rested his forehead against hers. He sighed. "I will enjoy the memory of this time," he said surprisingly.

She raised both eyebrows. "I thought you were brought into this relationship kicking and screaming, figuratively speaking," she commented. "You were reluctant at best and angry that it required such subterfuge to save Chacon and the princess from being killed."

He grimaced. "Personal relationships are difficult for me," he confided.

She slid her arms up around his neck and smiled at him. "Not to worry, sir, I'll take very good care of you and teach you everything you need to know about how to survive one."

He burst out laughing. "Which of us is the student here?" he asked outrageously.

She made a huffy sound. "I've been watching vids about how to be graceful and diplomatic and nurturing," she said. "I admit it was easier learning to pop enemy targets with a sniper kit, but never fear, I'll get the hang of it before we get to Benaski Port. Sfilla's a very good tutor."

He studied her, musing about how difficult it would be if she had to truly be his consort, instead of only pretending. Her life would be one endless round of diplomacy and détente.

"You're brooding again, sir," she accused.

He bent and brushed his cheek against hers. "You must learn not to call me sir," he cautioned.

"Many Cehn-Tahr women refer to their mates as 'sir,'" she replied audaciously. "I'll just be following protocol. Ask anyone." She cleared her throat. "Well, ask Sfilla, she's the one who told me." She studied him. "You know, Sfilla doesn't strike me as a cook."

He struggled not to let his face register anything except pleasant affection. "She is quite a good one."

She shrugged. "I guess so. There's just something about her…"

He hugged her tight. "You must not miss your lessons in High Cehn-Tahr," he said, letting her go. "You will be required to speak it when we go out among crowds at Benaski Port."

She made a face. "It's like talking with a mouth full of water."

He lifted an eyebrow.

"Sorry. It's an elegant dialect. But my tongue isn't accustomed to making such sounds."

"You are quite adept at it," he said with gentle praise. He smiled. "Sfilla is proud of your progress."

She laughed. "Good thing I only have to pretend to be obedient," she said, lowering her eyes.

"I must agree," he retorted. "Obedience is a word not in your vocabulary."

"I obey occasionally," she protested.

He was recalling that she'd leaped from a cliff, blindly, thinking she would certainly die, when he saved her from killing fall on Lagana, a planet which shared the same name as its principal continent. It had touched him deeply that she trusted him so much. He frowned.

"You're doing it again."

"Doing what?" he asked.

"Brooding."

He sighed. "Force of habit."

"I'll obey when it's necessary," she promised.

"When it suits your mood," he returned.

She flashed a grin at him.

He shook his head and walked away. She watched him go with affectionate amusement. These were precious days. She was sorry that she wouldn't remember them when the mission was over. On the other hand, she told herself, hope died hard.

"It's the last thing we lose," she thought to herself. "The very last thing."

He heard the thoughts in her mind, but he didn't speak. There was nothing more to be said. He knew that no power in the universe would make it possible for them to stay together. Even hope died when faced with an inheritance such as his.

CHAPTER FIVE

DTIMUN WAS WORRIED about Madeline. Her health had been less than perfect since the pregnancy began, and she still had the aftereffects of the crash on Akaashe to deal with. Had the curious Nagaashe not wanted to understand the incursion into their space, and eased the damaged ship to the ground, there would certainly have been no survivors of the crash. But that damage, added to the pressure of trying to perform an undercover mission, with the stress of possible discovery and death, was always present. Even such a short time into her pregnancy, her belly was swollen and she was having some of the more debilitating symptoms of the condition. She tried to hide them from him, but he knew.

Their accommodations on the civilian starcruiser were luxurious. They had two suites, one for Dtimun and one for Madeline. She shared hers with Sfilla. She had the best food and drink, the finest bed, the most elegant clothing that could be had in the civilized universe. But she was unnaturally quiet. Dtimun had become used to her flights of humor, her outrageous behavior, her lack of convention. But this pregnant human female was a different person altogether. He watched her when she was unaware; he accessed her thoughts carefully and covertly. Her outward calm was a front. She was frightened and sad. She wanted the child. He knew that this was, for her, an unforeseen complication. It had been her choice to regress the child and have the memory of her time with Dtimun, all of it, permanently wiped.

But that decision was torturing her. He knew, and did not trespass on her thoughts. But it saddened him, too. He had not expected to want the child, or its mother, so much.

He paced his quarters, ignoring the flash channel on the vidmaker. In fact, he switched it off impatiently and disabled the link. Distractions slowed his mind.

He became aware suddenly of an intrusion. It was cautious, and respectful. But it was there.

He looked at the wall while his mind pictured an old grizzled face with thick white hair. For one instant, he felt a real and chilling premonition. The child and his relationship with its human mother was a capital crime...

"No," the old fellow said in his mind, very gently. "You have nothing to fear from me. I do not approve of what you are doing. It is far too dangerous. But I will never betray you."

Dtimun felt a shock at the statement. "We are breaking many laws," he thought back.

There was a brief laugh. "Your mother and I broke many more, in the old days. This is the sort of thing we would have done, in your place." He became somber. "Komak told me more than he told you. I know where you are going, and why, and what you have to accomplish to insure the future."

"Komak is related to us."

The old one laughed in his mind. "You sound quite certain of this."

"He was a telepath. Only our Clan is so gifted."

"Yes, but in the future there will be much mingling of genetic material," came the amused reply. "You have no idea what changes will come from the warwoman's accident on Akaashe. She truly carries the future inside her, as your mother has said."

"You are speaking to my mother?" Dtimun asked amusedly.

"Quite often. We are concerned for your safety, and that of your mate and your child."

Dtimun's teeth ground together. "She is not well."

"Caneese has given instructions to Dr. Hahnson, who provided the medicines the warwoman is taking. Komak assured me that they would be effective, and that she would survive the pregnancy."

Dtimun relaxed a little. "It was unexpected."

"What was?"

He shifted and moved away to the vidport, to look outside at the passing stars. "My...feelings for her, and the child."

"You want him, too."

He closed his eyes. He did not need to say the words. His father was quite adept at reading them in his mind, when his son was unable to block them. Strong emotion made it difficult to hide turbulence.

"Yes," Dtimun said finally. "I want him very much."

There was a pause. "You and I have been at odds for decades over an incident that you did not truly understand. Will you listen, if I tell you the truth of it?"

Dtimun sighed and sat down in a comfortable chair. "Yes," he said after a minute, and felt the old one's pleasure in the word.

"This is what truly happened," came the grim reply. And an explanation was tendered that Dtimun had never considered possible. It came as a shock, and not a pleasant one.

Dtimun's perfect romance of the past took on new dimensions. He had idealized a woman whom the former Rojok dictator, Mangus Lo, had sent to assassinate him. His father's intervention had spared his life. Nor had he killed the woman deliberately. She had come at him with a small poisoned silver dagger, the sort used by assassins. He had carried no weapon and thought the *kehmatemer* had secured the woman, but she freed herself and meant to kill him. He had grabbed a sword from the wall display only just in time to protect himself.

The old one hesitated. "You know that she was not pregnant," he said with some surprise.

"Yes. Since I felt my child in Madeline's womb," Dtimun replied. "I knew nothing of pregnancy in those days. I accepted what the Dacerian woman told me." He sounded bitter. "I thought I loved her. But I know the difference, now."

"You were young. Of all our children, you were the most sheltered," he added solemnly. "Alkaasar was groomed to be my heir. My youngest son would have been given a military command, at some point. But most of my hopes rested in you, as the most able military commander of our empire."

Dtimun was caught by surprise at the praise.

"Your theories of command, your combat strategies, are taught even at the Tri-Galaxy Military Academy," the old one continued. "You have surpassed my greatest expectations. Of my three sons, it is of you that I am most proud."

Dtimun felt a jolt of emotion that he tried to hide.

The old one's voice smiled. "The warwoman does not

know what you risked to go to her rescue on Akaashe. One day she will. I value her, as the Nagaashe said when they contacted me. All of us do. You cannot think that I would permit the two of you to be put to death for breaking a stupid law."

There was surprise in Dtimun's silent thoughts. "Stupid?"

"Indeed," the old one replied. "And even now, change is being debated in the Dectat. There is a growing movement to offer citizenship to Ruszel for the miracle of the treaty with the Nagaashe, and to give her a military rank."

That was a bigger surprise. "You are using threats and intimidation to accomplish this," he accused.

The old one laughed. "I probably would, if it became necessary. But it was one of our more racist representatives who suggested it before I could. Ruszel is revered by the lawmakers. Even by my critics."

"My mother said that this is in line with the prophecy."

"I feel your mother's gentle touch in the fulfillment of this prophecy," the old one chuckled. "And Komak's. You must know that it would have been a simple matter to simulate a pregnancy for this operation."

Dtimun frowned. "Madeline mentioned it, but I felt it would be discovered and the mission lost."

"Caneese and Komak presented a united front and accomplished their goal with no interference at all. Such an event could not be hidden from me," he added smugly. "I know everything that happens in the empire."

"Yes," Dtimun answered. "You always have."

"However, since the law is still in place, and my..."

position…requires me to obey it, I can know nothing of the mission or the pregnancy or the bonding."

"I will remember," he replied with a smile in his tone.

"That being said," the old one continued, "I could not be more pleased at your choice of consort." He chuckled. "Komak was quite insistent that the true history of this time should be written, but I refused to let him publish some of my controversial actions. He said that my reticence in the future was responsible for his trip to this time."

"What specific controversial actions?" Dtimun asked, distracted.

"For one thing, contacting our most formidable enemy commander to bargain for Ruszel and her two subordinates on Akaashe, since we had no treaty with the Nagaashe. For another," he added, "my complicity in your efforts to save that same enemy commander from removal by his own emperor. The public, I fear, would not understand."

Dtimun nodded. "That is possible."

Dtimun got up and paced some more. "There are two other matters. She does not know the truth about us, or about me."

"She was willing to give her life to save yours," the old one reminded him gently. "And you think your true appearance would alter those feelings?"

"They very well could. You must remember what happened with the colony of humans. I can never forget."

The old one was sad. "A mistake, one of many I made in the early years, when I was learning how to command. It has colored our relationship with humans for many decades. But the humans of your Morcai Battalion revere you," the old one told him. "It will not matter to them. And it will certainly not matter to Ruszel, who has the heart of a galot."

"The inheritance laws…" Dtimun began.

"You are concerned that your son, who will be of mixed blood, will not inherit your lands and titles," the older alien interrupted. "I am trying to address this issue in the Dectat now."

A rush of pleasure accompanied the words. Dtimun had lived in grief and sorrow for many years, and not only because of the Dacerian woman's death. Now, he felt some sort of hope for a future he had not thought possible.

"She will have to live on Memcache," the old one continued. "Her Ambassador Taylor would find a way to have her spaced if she ever returned to Trimerius."

"Yes, I know." Dtimun's face set in hard lines. "I would like to snap his neck."

"Plans are in motion to deal with him," the old one said. "Do not interfere. You will be pleased at the end result."

Dtimun sighed. "Very well."

"It will mean a recognition of your true place in our government," the old fellow continued quietly. "A public one. And a public bonding ceremony. You will have to step down from command of the Holconcom, as well."

"I know." There was deep sadness in the words. "It is not that I mind the change. Madeline and the child will more than make up for the loss of command. But I had hoped that Komak would replace me one day," he said heavily. "I grew fond of him."

"So did we all. We will see him again," he added, and there was amusement in his tone.

"When?"

"Soon," came the reply. "But for now, as debate continues, you must not divulge what I have told you. I am not here. You told me nothing. I have no knowledge of your bonding or the child your mate carries."

Dtimun chuckled out loud. "Very well." He hesitated. "Madeline did not want a child," he said suddenly. "The regression and the mind wipe were her own solution."

"You should try harder to penetrate her mind," the old fellow told him. "She sings to the child in some strange ancient human tongue. She weeps when you do not see her. She mourns the child already, as she mourns you. She expects to go back to the Amazon Division when this mission is over, and into a forward unit, where she hopes to die…"

"What?"

"…to die, in order to free you from the bonding so that you can take another mate, a Cehn-Tahr mate whose child can inherit your lands and titles," the old fellow continued after the interruption. "Even now, she seeks to protect you from what she thinks of as the stigma of fathering a child onto a human female."

"That is absurd!" Dtimun burst out. "There is no stigma…!"

"I am telling you her thoughts. She will block you from seeing them. She has had help, learning to block telepaths. Do not ask, I will not reveal her confidant," he added before Dtimun could speak. "She will do what she thinks is best to save your career and your life."

"I will lock her in a closet and swallow the key," Dtimun said haughtily.

The old fellow roared with laughter. "There is an

easier way. Tell her how you feel. You hide it so well that she has no idea that you want her or the child."

Dtimun shifted restlessly. "I was taught from childhood never to display emotion, lest enemies in the Dectat saw my feelings and used them for their own agenda."

"It was a lesson well learned, and valuable," the old one replied. "I had to learn it the hard way. My feelings for your mother were used to coax me into policies I detested. When I learned that I was betraying myself, I became adept at concealing my true feelings in public."

"Indeed."

The old one laughed. "Yes, I have even concealed them from you and Caneese, and my other children. You are the last of our line," he continued. "I had thought that a lesser member of the aristocracy must one day take your place in the inheritance, because you refused to breed. But your choice of mates is magnificent. And the future will be remarkable, because of your child's influence." There was a deep chuckle. "And he will not be the only child."

Dtimun's breath caught. "With Madeline?"

"Of course."

Dtimun felt the impact of emotion like a blow. He sat down on the edge of his desk. He had never considered that there might be even one child. And now...

"A warrior should have many children," the old fellow said. "Male and female. But he should spend time with them, give them affection and guidance, and love them. I have failed terribly in this regard. My aim was conquest, and I sacrificed everything and everyone dear to me in that goal. My regrets are legion, my sorrows without number. I grieve for my dead children, and my lack of insight that might have spared them in the flower of adulthood."

Dtimun had a faraway look in his eyes, which were a somber blue. "Komak was fond of blaming fate for these tragedies. Karamesh, he called it. He had a philosophical outlook which I lack."

"He is a student of many fields, and an expert in some. His accomplishments will revolutionize our world, and many other worlds. He will be quite famous in the future."

"Who is he?"

There was a pause. "I will tell you, when the time comes. It has not, yet. First things first. You must maintain contact with me covertly. I will help, if I can."

"I am grateful."

"You take great risks, you and the warwoman, for an enemy."

"Chacon was never that, personally."

"I know. It grieves me that we find ourselves in opposite camps," the old one told him. "Chacon will eventually overthrow his government, however, and unite his people with the Cehn-Tahr."

"You have been listening to Caneese's prophecies," Dtimun chuckled.

"No. I have been listening to Komak," came the dry reply.

"He told me very little."

"He did not dare," the old fellow replied. "The future is not set in stone. It can be altered. He told me the timeline and made me promise not to interfere in any of this. I could only get him to agree to let me contact you and provide help when I could. This he permitted, and he did finally understand why I concealed public knowledge of my part in these actions."

"It is a strange concept, making the future."

"Very strange. But if you succeed, the future is assured." He paused again. "You must take great care of your mate and my grandchild. Caneese and I are quite excited."

Dtimun laughed. "So am I."

"Do not let the warwoman out of your sight."

"You may depend on that."

"And take great care of yourself, as well," came a quieter, more intense admonition. "We have been at odds for decades. But there was never a time when I did not love you, or wish you well. You are my only son. I...could not bear to give you up."

Dtimun bit his lip and tried to conceal the rush of emotion the confession drew from him. He was not successful.

"And do not offer to trade the warwoman for a Yo-muth at Benaski Port!" came a gruffer, humorous addition.

Dtimun laughed. "It was a joke. I would never have done it." He paused. "Lawson will find it difficult to pursue his combat strategies, now that I have withdrawn the Holconcom. I am certain that it has caused great anguish in the Council. But it was the only way I could get around Ambassador Taylor's orders, and to save Madeline. The humans give their ambassadors more power than even their political leaders."

"I know that. The Dectat knew, also, and your actions were approved. As it happens, they produced a grand result, the treaty with the Nagaashe. No one will oppose your bonding in the Dectat now. In fact, it will be acclaimed."

Dtimun sighed. "I am in your debt."

"Of course you are. I am your father," came the smug reply. "Let this be a lesson to you. As when you were very young, you cannot hide things from me."

"In the future, I will not try to."

"Wise thinking. We will speak again. Walk with care."

And he was gone.

DTIMUN WONDERED WHETHER or not to share his conversation with his father with Madeline, and decided against it. His father was risking a great deal to offer him support, even in his position. One innocent slip of the tongue could make much mischief. He couldn't risk that. Not yet.

CHAPTER SIX

BENASKI PORT WAS built on an asteroid in the Catarus Belt, as it was called locally, a point roughly midway between the planetary systems of the Cehn-Tahr Empire and the Tri-Galaxy Council of Planets. It was the most lawless place known to humanoid life-forms, because no formal law existed there. There was Port Security, but it was a joke; its officials could and did take bribes.

Outlaws and outcasts, pirates and their pursuers, diplomats and beggars, lived in a colorful neon jungle of light and shadow, all situated under a huge glass bubble on the asteroid's surface. Glass, on a terrestrial planet, would shatter easily. But on an airless moon or asteroid, it attained the strength of steel.

There were cheap apartments midtown and luxurious dwellings on the outskirts of the city, near the spaceport. It was to the latter that the skimmer delivered Dtimun, Madeline and Sfilla.

"I will handle all the arrangements," Sfilla assured them, climbing out first. She ran toward the main building of the small complex. There were artificial plants and flowers in stone planters, and a holopond, complete with CGI fish. It looked very real. Madeline almost trailed her fingers through the "water" before she realized what she was doing.

Dtimun, indulgent, smiled at her. "Even in an artificial atmosphere, the gravity here would be too uncomfortable for fish."

"I should have known that." She smiled shyly.

He looked at her with pure male appreciation of her obvious pregnancy under the pretty blue robes she wore.

"Is my nose on crooked?" she asked self-consciously.

"Certainly not. I was thinking that pregnancy suits you," he added in a soft, deep tone.

She flushed a little. It was difficult, this new relationship. And still harder to reconcile the humanoid male in front of her with the taciturn commander of the past few years.

He moved closer. "It is difficult for me, as well," he confessed. "Our relationship, while turbulent, has always been nonphysical."

"I never thought of males as anything but comrades," she tried to explain. "I was honest when I told you, at the beginning, that I had no idea what was normal female behavior."

"I believe you are better informed now," he said, and although he didn't smile, his lack of expression was suspicious.

"Sir!" she said with mock embarrassment. Then she spoiled it by grinning wickedly.

He chuckled and turned away. Sfilla was returning. "It is just up here," she said. "They will bring our luggage presently." She led the way.

THE SUITE WAS EXQUISITE. Madeline had never known luxury, until she arrived at the fortress on Memcache. This was almost as opulent. There were chairs and loungers everywhere, at least two of which were antigrav chairs, which could be moved to any location by means of switches on the armpads. There was a high deck with artificial plants and flowers, and a low deck with a pool.

"The water in that one is real," Dtimun told her. "It has temperature control and jets for massage."

She stared at it, entranced. "I've never been deliberately immersed in water in my life," she said. That was true. Recycled chemical showers took the place of water on ships. She glanced at him, grinning. "I don't think being thrown into a mud hole by an enemy soldier counts."

He laughed. "It does not."

"What would one wear in that?" she wondered, indicating the pool.

He was silent.

She turned back and stared at him until she got the message, and then she chuckled. "I'm going to check out the kitchen." She escaped to the sound of deep laughter.

Sfilla joined her. She laughed, too. "He would never enter such a body of water unclothed with a female," she whispered to Madeline. "No Cehn-Tahr male would. It would be, how do you humans say, indiscreet."

"Really?" Madeline was impressed.

"Just as you are discreet, so is he," Sfilla said gently. She studied Madeline's glowing complexion curiously. "He is so different with you. In all my years with the family, I have rarely heard him laugh, or seen him happy."

Madeline smiled at her. "I drive him nuts on the ship," she pointed out.

"Nuts?"

"Crazy," Madeline told her. "I don't mean to. It just seems to happen."

Sfilla shook her head. "A female on a warship. It is a strange concept."

"Wearing robes is a strange concept," she countered. "I've worn a uniform since I was about three years old."

"That is sad," Sfilla said.

"It was exciting, though. I learned to use a sniper kit my first year in the military. I was incredibly gifted, they said."

"Gifted." Sfilla managed to look shocked. It was a deliberate expression, behind which a smile lurked that Madeline did not notice.

"I know," Madeline said gently. "It's a strange concept. What do we have to eat? I'm starving!"

"That is the influence of the child," the Cehn-Tahr woman said gently. "He grows quite fast."

"I have noticed," Madeline said, one hand resting on the firm mound of her belly. She smoothed her fingers over it absently, wondering what her child would look like, if he would favor her or Dtimun more. Then she realized that she would never know, and the sadness swept over her like a cold wave.

Sfilla noticed the change of expression, but she didn't say anything. She went to make food.

Dtimun came up behind Madeline. His lean hands caught her shoulders. "You must not think of it," he said quietly.

"I know. It's hard, that's all." She turned and looked up at him with wide, soft eyes. "I didn't understand what it would be like, to carry a child. It's very different, the reality."

He took her face in his hands and bent to lay his forehead gently against hers. "Very different," he agreed.

She drew in a long breath. Her hands rested softly

on the front of his robe, against his broad chest. "I'm so tired," she said.

"That is the influence of the child," he said with affection.

She opened her eyes and lifted her head. She wondered if he was comparing this pregnancy with the one before, that of the woman he loved.

"In fact, I was not," he said softly. His face tautened. "She was not pregnant. And I never knew it, until I felt the child inside you. For decades, I blamed your old fellow for her death and the loss of my child. Only now am I certain that she never carried one."

Her heart jumped. "But you said...!"

"She told me there was to be a child," he replied. "I understood nothing about pregnancy. Now I know the difference."

She was thinking that if the woman lied about her pregnancy, she might have lied about other things.

"Yes," he said aloud.

He let her go and moved away, troubled by his own thoughts.

Madeline watched him in silence. She couldn't think of anything to say that would help. That realization must have been very painful for him.

She was grateful for Sfilla's covert tutoring. She hadn't realized that the Cehn-Tahr woman was a minor telepath until their last day on Memcache, when she had slipped and revealed it. That had allowed Madeline to ask her for help, to block the commander from her thoughts. Some of them were disturbing.

She had in mind going back to the Amazon Division as soon as this mission was over. She didn't want him aware of her plans. If it ever became known that Madeline had been pregnant with his child, he would be disgraced, and she was determined to keep the secret. Even with the memory wipe, a detailed physical scan would reveal that there had been a pregnancy. She couldn't risk Dtimun's career, or his life, again. She would arrange her affairs so that when they returned, she could report immediately to Admiral Mashita. And Dtimun would not know, until it was too late. She placed her hand on the small mound of her belly and felt the pain all the way to her soul.

THAT NIGHT, SHE stood on the balcony overlooking the Silken Strip in the distance, the loop of neon lights that seemed to go on forever. On the bleak asteroid, it was a band of color and life.

There was no real atmosphere, except what was created under the blister dome that contained the outpost, but she felt something like wind whip her hair away from her face. Her life had never been so complicated. This tiny being inside her was causing her to feel things she'd never imagined.

Dtimun joined her. "You must not brood over the future," he said firmly. "It only distorts the present."

"Yes, well, I don't imagine you've ever been pregnant, sir, so you won't be able to see my point of view."

He chuckled unexpectedly. "No. I have not."

She laughed softly, trying to imagine that outlandish scenario.

He drew her against him and held her there, his arms around her. "Tomorrow, we must start making inquiries," he said against her hair. "If the two we seek are actually here, it should not be too difficult to find them."

She was enjoying the closeness. Her life had been

one of solitude, apartness. It was disturbing to find how much she liked being close to him.

He lifted his head and searched her eyes in the dim light on the balcony. His own eyes were a solemn blue. "You see things from a perspective which is not accurate," he said suddenly. "I am not as you see me, Madeline. There are secrets I keep, even now."

"Why?"

"It will do no good to discuss them," he said flatly. "What is, is."

"And that is as clear as mud," she muttered.

"A good analogy," he replied.

"Smoke and mirrors is a better one," she said with a little of her old mischief. "You thought the humans would feel threatened if they knew how powerful your mind was, or how you fought. You were wrong. Your crew would follow you off a cliff. I certainly would."

He traced her fine eyebrows. "The Cehn-Tahr have other traits, of which we never speak."

"This would have something to do with why the mating was in the dark and I wasn't supposed to touch you," she guessed, nodding when he lifted an eyebrow in surprise. "But I said at the time that my instruments and my senses told a different story about your physical makeup. I know you aren't what you seem."

"We do not reveal ourselves to outworlders."

"I'm not. I have temporary Cehn-Tahr citizenship and we are bonded," she reminded him.

"Bonded for a mission, Madeline," he replied quietly. "Only for a space of days or weeks, however long it takes us to perform the task which brought us here. As you yourself wished, when we return, you will regress the child and have a short-term memory wipe. You will not remember any of this."

Her heart fell to her knees. She went cold in his arms. Yes, it had been her own request, one which she now regretted with all her heart.

"That makes no difference, either," he said softly. He could read her surface thoughts quite accurately. Strange, how difficult it was to see deeper. He recalled his father's comment that she had been tutored in mind blocks. But there were few Cehn-Tahr who could have provided such counseling. He wondered who it was.

"Our laws are absolute," he added grimly, after a minute. "Even were the Species Act overturned, the inheritance laws are very much in place. No child of an outworlder will ever be able to inherit my titles or my lands. That is the law."

She felt vaguely nauseated. She often forgot the difference in their stations in life. He was an aristocrat. She was a very lowly human soldier. She knew that it would be impossible for them to have the child, at any rate. Discovery would mean death, for both of them. She tried not to think of the future. But it pushed its way into the present constantly. She stepped away from him. "Sorry, sir," she said formally. "I wasn't thinking clearly."

He scowled. "Madeline, I did not mean it that way. Your social status has nothing to do with this."

She managed a smile. "Yes, but we're very different in background. Even if there were no laws, it would still be impossible. I'm going in. Sleep well, sir."

She turned and left him there, biting his own tongue for what he should never have put into words. He had not meant to hurt her. It was difficult, this changed status between them.

DAYS PASSED IN their search for Chacon. It was a small community, but it was quite possible for even a famous military commander to be hidden there. Dtimun was occupied with contacts who might be able to ascertain Chacon's whereabouts.

Meanwhile, Madeline had made friends with an elderly retired soldier who was living in the hotel she and Dtimun occupied. His name was Mardol, and he had all sorts of souvenirs of the battles he'd fought. One was an ancient sniper rifle, which was his pride and joy. He didn't know Madeline's background, but when he told her about it, she showed interest in it.

She went with him to his quarters. He motioned her into his one good chair and pulled a heavy metal box out from under the sofa which doubled as his bunk. He opened it, displaying the vintage weapon.

"A Calback 220 Armonium sniper rifle!" she exclaimed. The old weapon was familiar to her. During her first assignment, as an eight-year-old, she had won medals for her abilities as a sharpshooter. She was placed in strategic locations during battles to thin out the forward enemy patrols. Her skills as a sniper were formidable.

The old soldier gaped at her. "Why, yes," he said, surprised.

"It's in beautiful condition," she said, staring at it.

"I have not used it in many years," he said, "but I keep it properly cleaned."

"There's no power pack," she pointed out.

He chuckled. "I have no need of one. However, this weapon was made for innovations. It can use any power pack, including one from a *chasat*. What a pity they replaced it with that Ararom 520 sightscope. This was efficiency at its best. They said it was too heavy." He scoffed. "Too heavy! The weight gave it stability! The least recoil can cost you a hit at great distances." He sighed. "Well, the old ways are gone. I suppose it is as well that the old weapons are gone, too." He closed the box and studied her. "How odd, to find a female who enjoys talk of war and weapons. How did you know the model of the rifle?"

"My father is in the military," she said, smiling. "I learned a lot from him, about weapons."

"I see. Was he attached to a sniper unit?" he asked.

"To a forward commando division, but not artillery. He's an airman."

"A fine assignment," the old man said. "It is a great pity, to grow too old to be useful in war. I do miss the front lines, Lady Maltiche," he added, using the name she was called by covertly.

So do I, she thought, but she didn't say it. "Could you tell me again about that battle at Lefor Galt?" she asked instead. "It was quite exciting!"

He chuckled and put the gun away. "It would be my pleasure."

DTIMUN FOUND HER still listening to the old man recite his combat history. He excused himself and said that Madeline must come to dinner with him.

"You are fortunate to have so knowledgeable a bonded companion," the old soldier told him. He smiled and shook his head. "I can understand why the two of you are here, in this place. You would surely die for your present condition, Lady Maltiche. It is only that I do not understand how you were able to breed…" He stopped at Dtimun's expression. He said. "Forgive me.

The modern world has passed me by. I suppose the advances in biotech have been impressive. I have never heard of a Cehn-Tahr child which is part human."

"Nor has anyone else," Madeline laughed. "It will be a first."

"Indeed. A pity you must live here," the old man said, his smile fading. "It is not a place to raise a child. They say the colonies on the Rim have persons who are outcast from their own societies. Might you not be able to settle there, beyond the reach of your respective governments?"

"That is a possibility," Dtimun replied quietly.

"It is sad when people who wish to be together are denied only for political reasons," the old soldier said. "Still, there are ways around the law." He chuckled. "I know. I have found most of them."

Madeline laughed. So did Dtimun. "We must go." He held out his hand and Madeline slid hers into it.

"I enjoy our conversations," she told the old man.

"I enjoy them even more. There are not many persons who oblige an old warrior by asking to hear his tales of valor. You are a kind young woman."

"I do not oblige you," she pointed out. "I really enjoy the stories."

"Come back anytime," he told her. "You will be welcome." He glanced at Dtimun. "She knows a sniper kit when she sees one. She even knew the model!"

"I told him that my father was in the military," Madeline said quickly.

"Indeed. Good day," he told the old man respectfully.

"Good day."

Dtimun led her back out into the hall, but he didn't

let go of her hand. "How is it that you are familiar with sniper rifles?" he queried.

She grinned. "My first assignment was as a sniper," she told him. "I had the highest score in the division."

"How old were you?"

"Eight," she said.

He frowned. Even the Cehn-Tahr military did not accept boys until they were adolescent. "You had no childhood at all."

She flushed. "Well, we do what the state says we must," she told him. "Does Sfilla have the meal prepared already? I'm starved."

"She does." He studied her quietly. "You do not like discussing your past."

She grimaced. "It was regimented. I love the military," she added. "But it does seem improper to take children at such a young age and teach them how to kill." She shrugged, her eyes somber. "The Rojoks do it as well, though. Perhaps both races are barbaric."

He smiled. His fingers touched her cheek lightly. "War creates such barbarity." The smile faded. "The Cehn-Tahr, in our first days as an empire, practiced much worse barbarity than your own race."

"Your emperor did what he thought was best to secure the empire," she said simply. "Politics and military decisions very seldom mesh."

He nodded.

Her hand rested gently on her stomach. Her eyes were sad. "If the child could be born," she said hesitantly, "I wouldn't wish him a childhood like mine."

He smoothed his hand over her hair. "My own was quite regimented. Each day had its own strict routine. I would not wish the child to follow such a pattern as my

own." He smiled sadly. "In a different life, perhaps…"
He let the thought trail away. His hand went back to his
side. "We should go in."

She nodded. She went ahead of him down the corridor, past the crowded, busy shops with their duty
free merchandise. Despite the danger of their situation, she enjoyed her pregnancy and the vast change
in her turbulent relationship with her commander. She
had never thought such things would be possible. She
hadn't wanted to think about a child at all. Now, the
child was the center of her world, and soon she would
be forced to put it away, as she put away other dreams
and hopes that were impossible.

"All things are possible, Madeline," he said in her
mind. There was a mysterious joy in the mental whisper that puzzled her.

But Sfilla was already at the transport, motioning for
them to hurry as she looked worriedly around.

"She thinks we're going to be captured and tor-
tured," Madeline thought wickedly. "She sees plots
everywhere."

"Humor her," he said. "She is a fine cook."

"I have to agree." She'd never cooked anything in her
life, except for assorted exotic wildlife over campfires
when on campaign. Food served a purpose—it wasn't
supposed to be enjoyable.

Sfilla's dishes were spicy and flavorful and truly
wonderful to eat. Madeline thought that she was growing far too used to gourmet living. It would be difficult
to go back to soldiering, now, after even this brief inter-
lude. Her mind set had changed, and she had softened,
in a way, become more vulnerable.

"It is the child which makes you feel vulnerable,"

he said gently, still in her mind. "The influence of hormones."

She laughed softly. "I suppose so." She glanced up at him as they neared the transport. He was very handsome. She thought that she would never tire of looking at him.

He glanced at her and his eyes went green. She flushed and ran ahead, to dive into the transport ahead of him. She really had to spend more time working on her mind blocks. And soon!

IN THE NIGHT, the child moved with fury. Another growth spurt bent her over double in the bed. It frightened her. She had never felt so alone, or so afraid. She got out of bed and looked out the insulated window, one hand on the child as she fought down her fear. It would be all right. She'd taken the drug Caneese had made for her. It would work. The child would be all right.

The pain came again. She closed her eyes against it. She was a combat soldier. She'd seen death, even dealt it early in her military career. It was absurd, to feel so frightened, especially for a child she could not even keep.

The air in the room stirred behind her, and she felt Dtimun's hands on her shoulders before she knew of his presence. She jumped involuntarily.

"Forgive me," he said gently as he turned her. "I did not mean to startle you."

He moved like a cat, she thought. He was wearing a sort of pant-skirt, like the Kahn-Bo uniform the Cehn-Tahr wore when they sparred aboard ship, except of a softer fabric, and his feet and his broad, muscular chest were bare. It was the way he had been dressed in the mating chamber just before the physicians arrived. Her eyes registered how attractive he was, although she tried not to let it show.

He was looking, too. Her long, reddish-gold hair curled around her face and over her shoulders. In the soft blue sleeping robe she wore, she looked younger.

"The child's movements disturb you," he said in his deep voice, while somber blue eyes looked down into her green ones. "But you bear the uneasiness alone, thinking it a weakness to seek comfort from me."

She looked straight ahead, at the thick hair wedged over the muscular, pale gold skin of his chest. "I'm all right." She shifted. "I know that Cehn-Tahr males don't share a room with their mates."

He raised an eyebrow arrogantly. "Sfilla has been talking to you," he said with faint disapproval.

"It's okay, sir," she said with a hint of her old mischief. "I told her that she must not share details of familial behavior with me, because I was an outworlder. She looked quite shocked."

He shook his head. His eyes flashed green. "I would have told you, had you asked. However, since you and I have broken so many protocols of behavior already, I hardly think one more will matter."

And as he spoke, he bent and scooped her up in his arms and carried her back to his own suite of rooms without another word.

He placed her on the huge round bed with its luxurious Yomuth-hair cover and propped her up against several silken pillows at the carved imported Seti marble headboard. "Move over," he said, and he climbed in beside her to sit, cross-legged, beside her.

He reactivated his virtual displays and was immediately surrounded by colorful controls and a vortex that resolved into a weapon.

"That's a VX3-Mexcache," she murmured, indicating the rapid-fire rail gun.

His eyes twinkled. "I had forgotten your background in weapons tech," he said. "Yes. This is a prototype. I have been working on an improvement in the combustion chamber which will solve the repeated overheating during rapid fire."

She was surprised. "I thought your training was military, sir."

He lifted an eyebrow. "Are you going to continue to refer to me as 'sir'?"

"Well, yes," she replied. "After all, this is only a temporary mission."

He shook his head and sighed. "My early training was in quantum mechanics and biochemistry," he told her. "I have doctorates in both fields."

She lay back on her pillows and studied him with quiet pride. "You never spoke of your education."

"There was no reason to." He manipulated the image and turned it, magnifying it, to bring up the combustion chamber, which was an emerillium-based trigger mechanism.

She turned, so that her shoulder and cheek rested on the mound of pillows. "You said that we'd broken behavioral protocols," she recalled frowning. "Which ones? If I'm allowed to ask."

"The first mating, as I explained to you, is only to prove fertility." He glanced at her and lifted an eyebrow over green eyes. "We are not permitted to take pleasure from it."

She cleared her throat and avoided his eyes. "Yes,

well, how would anyone know what happened except us?"

"The eldest of the court physicians is a minor royal who thinks herself a telepath," he continued. "She took exception to the length of time we spent in the mating chamber."

"I didn't realize." It hadn't seemed like a long time.

"She also commented on the placement of your wounds, and the fact that I remained during the examination," he added, his eyes showing a hint of the anger he had felt. "I sent her out the door with her belongings." He chuckled. "Caneese almost cheered. She was not fond of her, but she has too soft a heart to manage staff. She has since been replaced by a younger healer." He glanced at her. "She liked you."

"I don't remember much about the examination," she confessed.

He liked the soft blush on her cheeks, but not the memory of the violence and aggression he could not control at the beginning. His hand paused on the virtual controls. "It is feline behavior, the violence. While the galots can also be passionate, their first matings are brutal."

"We are all prisoners of our genetics," she said philosophically.

He glanced at her. "Perhaps we are."

She closed her eyes and snuggled closer into the pillows. "You didn't purr," she said with a wicked smile.

He pursed his lips and looked at her with twinkling green eyes. "No. The first mating is only to prove fertility. It is brutal, and brief. The second, however, after the birth of the first child, lasts for several days."

She gaped at him. "Days?"

He nodded. "Days. Our females do not have cycles of estrus as humans do. It must be induced, which is accomplished by mating."

Never having treated Cehn-Tahr females, Madeline was fascinated with this new information. She raised up on an elbow. "We have access to so little information about your species," she confessed. "I had to threaten Hahnson just to find out that the birth weight of Cehn-Tahr babies is about three times that of human ones." She frowned. "I think you're much larger than you appear. I know your weight is disproportionate to how you look."

He nodded. "We keep secrets."

"I wouldn't be afraid of you," she pointed out.

He only smiled. "Words."

She sighed. He wasn't going to budge. "But each mating produces a child?"

He nodded. "Another hard-wired trait. Family is everything to us."

She was sad. She felt the child inside her moving again and she grimaced at the discomfort.

He looked over at her. "The child is very restless."

"I think he's complaining about his accommodations," she laughed. "He wants more room."

His eyes smiled at her. She looked at home in his bed.

"You don't have to keep me in here," she said drowsily. "I know the Cehn-Tahr don't sleep as humans do."

"I can adjust my rhythms to yours," he said easily. He frowned. "I do not like the idea of having you apart from me at night. My mind is linked to yours, but distractions sometimes occur. I will rest easier if you are close."

"I was just thinking the same thing, from my point

of view." Her eyes opened, soft and hungry. "I wonder which one of us the child would have favored."

"Your background in genetics is superior to mine," he pointed out. "Speculate."

"I think he would look more like you. I don't know about his eyes, if they would change color, as yours do."

She felt sad as she realized that the speculation was a moot point. They would never see the child born.

"You don't think the old fellow knows we're here?" she worried. "I hope he doesn't try to read my mind. But, then, it wouldn't work across so many parsecs, would it?"

"There are no barriers of time and space that would prevent him," he said surprisingly. "He once blew up a small attack monofighter from miles away. It would have killed me, had he not been so quick."

She sat up. "On Ondar, when I decoyed the Rojok guards at their outpost, one of their officers was about to shoot me." The anger and shock on his face were briefly disconcerting, and flattering, but she continued, "I heard a voice in my mind, telling me to throw the sensor net over me. I did, and the enemy soldier gasped and died although I didn't touch him. Then, when I escaped, a Rojok strafe ship came after me. It suddenly exploded. I never knew who saved me, or how." Her eyes softened. "It must have been him. Nobody else could have done it."

He smiled. "He is fond of you."

She sighed, and put her hand on her belly. "If he could see me now, I'll bet he wouldn't be. And he's in the Dectat." She winced. "I guess if he found out, he'd have a front row seat at our spacings."

"I wonder," he mused, without revealing what he

knew. "His attitudes have undergone a conversion of late."

She leaned back and moved restlessly. The child's shifting was a little painful. "I wonder if I could use a sedative without affecting him," she wondered, sliding open the panel over her wrist unit. "Perhaps a very mild one."

"Is it painful?"

She nodded. "Very. I won't sleep if I don't do something." She frowned. "You took away the Altairian child's pain aboard ship, when we rescued the colonists on Terramer. But you couldn't take away mine, on Akaashe. The old fellow said that you were too—" She broke off, not wanting to say the words.

He turned to her. "He said that I was too emotionally involved with you. It is true," he added quietly. "It clouds my abilities in the matter of healing."

She wanted to pursue that subject, but she was too inhibited. She injected a mild sedative, one that would not linger in her system, and felt the pain slowly subside. "The old fellow is your father."

His eyes darkened. "A guess?"

"An educated one. I saw in his mind that he once courted Caneese with a pot of *canolithe*," she added, her tone soft and becoming drowsy. "Were they bonded?"

He hesitated, but only briefly. "Yes."

She smiled. "He still loves her very much. I saw it in his mind." She looked up at him. "He led the Holconcom, when he was young."

His eyebrows lifted. "You saw a great deal during the mind link."

"Too much?" she wondered, smiling at his expression. "Not to worry. Hahnson is going to do a short-term memory wipe on me when we get back to Memcache. I won't remember any of it."

He was uncomfortable at the idea of the memory wipe. She would forget, also, that one day on Memcache when they had learned so much about each other. He studied his controls with eyes that did not see them. The child would also be gone. He would pass Madeline in the corridor and she would see him only as her commanding officer. There would be no more conversations. He shared things with her that he could not share with anyone else. He felt suddenly empty.

But then he recalled his conversation with his father, and the sadness passed. There was a future for him with Madeline and their child, but it would be dangerous to discuss it before this mission was over. He would have to keep his secrets, for the time being, even if they brought anguish to her. Revealing what he knew was far too dangerous to the Clan.

He turned to her. But she was already asleep. He touched her reddish-gold curls, moving them away from the soft skin of her face. She looked very feminine, very vulnerable. He wanted to protect her, to keep her close. It was the influence of the child, he was certain, that made him protective and possessive. But he had been protective of her almost from the start.

He frowned. He spent a great deal of time looking into her mind. On at least two occasions, he had influenced her dreams. Thinking about it made him uncomfortable. He shifted on the bed. She was his mate. He did not want to give her up. On the other hand, how were they to overcome the barriers? The most important was his true self, which she had never seen. He hated the idea of revealing himself to her, because she might, as many humans had, react with fear and distaste.

But even if he could overcome that obstacle, there were others, nonphysical but impossible to circumvent. His aristocratic status did not allow bonding with a non-Cehn-Tahr. Her child could not inherit. This was beside the fact that they would both be spaced, despite his heritage, if it were known to the Dectat that she carried his child. He averted his eyes and went back to his computations. Thinking about it did no good. His father seemed confident that these obstacles could be overcome. Dtimun was hopeful, but less certain. He glanced at her again and smiled. She was, he thought, quite unique. There must be a way to resolve the problems. He would find a way. He was not giving up his mate or his child, no matter what the consequences might be.

WHEN MADELINE AWOKE, Dtimun was already dressed and gone into the main part of town to talk to some shady characters he knew. Or so Sfilla related. He was looking for Chacon. They had to find him. Madeline wondered if Lyceria had made it safely to the port, and if she and Chacon had connected with each other. She smiled, recalling Chacon's hopeless attraction to the Cehn-Tahr woman, and hers for him. At least they had a chance of a long relationship, if they survived the war. An emperor's daughter would have choices denied to a poor soldier.

She ate breakfast and then took a skimmer into the port city, much to Sfilla's unease. The woman insisted on going with her. It was too dangerous a place for Madeline to go alone, she said. Madeline didn't remind her that she'd spent her life in dangerous places. It touched her that Sfilla was so concerned for her. The woman had placed a veil over her hair and face, to help disguise her. As if, Madeline thought, the encompassing robes didn't do enough of that already. Reddish-gold hair wasn't that rare, she argued, even Dacerian women had it in abundance. But she was overruled. She gave in with good grace. She was also advised to keep her eyes lowered. Green eyes were unknown in this part of the galaxy, even among Dacerians.

She paused at a shop that sold exotic silks, fascinated by a fabric that changed color with the temperature to which it was exposed. It sparkled with tiny energy particles that danced in its gossamer depths. It was a royal blue, flecked with gold, and totally exquisite. Madeline had never had a taste for expensive garments, but this fabric reminded her of the robes Dtimun had ordered woven for her the night they went to the Altair Embassy. She had felt uncomfortable at first, but then she felt proud at Dtimun's obvious delight in her manner of dress.

"If you like it," Sfilla told her, "we may purchase it. He—" meaning Dtimun "—gave me mems with which to buy anything that you desired."

"It's so beautiful," Madeline said, surprised at her own interest in fabric.

Sfilla smiled. "I can weave it into robes for you," she said. "I have my bag at the hotel, in which I carry my weaving tools."

"I would love to have it," she confessed.

Sfilla grinned. She turned to the shop owner, a Dacerian, and began the long process of bargaining for the best price. "This may take some time," she told Madeline. "There is a java shop across the way, there, if you wish to sit and sample Dacerian coffee while I am occupied here."

Coffee! Madeline's eyes twinkled as she saw the café, its patrons sipping from mugs. "I would love that," she confessed. The Cehn-Tahr did not drink coffee, so she'd missed her usual morning cups.

"I will find you there," Sfilla promised. "But stay in sight of me."

What an odd thing to say, Madeline thought, but she only smiled and nodded. As if she couldn't take care of herself! She was a combat veteran, while Sfilla cooked and kept the rooms in order. There was nothing wrong with that, but it amused Madeline that the other woman thought to protect her.

CHACON WAS FURIOUS. He pulled Lyceria into the back of a clothing shop whose owner he knew and closed the door.

"Why did you come here?" he demanded, glaring down at her from his slitted eyes.

"To see you," she faltered.

"Our people are at war," he raged at her. "You could be put to death by your own government as a traitor if it became known that you even had contact with me. We risk enough by sending flashes back and forth to one another."

"There is a plot to kidnap you," she began.

"There is always a plot of some sort," he interrupted.

"No! This one is serious," she insisted worriedly. "They dare not kill you because Chan Ho would be immediately suspected. But they can sell you into slavery. You will simply disappear without a trace!"

He sobered.

"There was no one I could tell who could have helped," she said, answering the question she saw in his mind. "And I would only have endangered any other Cehn-Tahr whom I involved. I did attempt to flash the warning to you, but I was concerned it might be intercepted, because sometimes I am monitored. It made no difference... I was never able to get through to you. Apparently whoever monitors you has become familiar with the signatures of my flashes and denied you access to them. This was a last resort." She looked down at his broad chest. "I could not bear to think of you in a mining colony...."

"Lyceria," he said in anguish. "This is impossible."

Her eyes looked up into his. They were a soft, opaque blue.

"Stop it," he muttered, and blocked her telepathic intrusion.

She blinked, surprised. "How can you do that?"

"I should not have to," he returned. "It is a breach of ethics to touch a mind without permission."

"Someone taught you," she guessed.

"Even among the Rojok there are telepaths," he said. "It has proven to be a valuable skill. Never in my career have I been more hunted. Chan Ho wishes to return to his late uncle's policies," he added grimly. "I will never permit it, as long as I am alive." He stared into her eyes. "Who is behind this attempt, do you know?"

"No," she confessed miserably. "My spies say that it is someone you trust, but nothing more."

"You could have flashed me, through a scrambled port," he said, his voice a little less accusing.

She searched his dusky face silently, her expression one of bitterness and sorrow. "Of course I could have."

She averted her eyes. "It has been a long time since you rescued me from Ahkmau."

"Not so very long."

Soft dark blue anguish colored her great eyes. "A lifetime." She stared at his broad chest. "You answer my flashes, but as though you dislike receiving them, and when you reply, it is with diplomatic formality."

"To protect you, you little fool," he shot back angrily, "in case they were intercepted. You risk much."

"I could not let them make a prisoner of you," she said miserably.

His thin lips made a straight line. He was flattered. More than flattered. But he clamped down hard on his emotions. "You must leave here at once."

She laughed with faint self-contempt. "That is no longer possible. My forged papers have been stolen. I am without proof of citizenship, although most would recognize me as Cehn-Tahr. But that will not give me access to a ship. Nor do I have funds. Those, too, were stolen."

He looked at her as if she'd suddenly sprouted feathers. "They followed you here."

Her face lost every drop of color.

"If there is a plot," he said softly, dangerously, "it included your own capture. It was baited and sprung." He drew her farther into the shop and looked around worriedly. "We must disguise you and hide you until I can think of some way to return you to your family."

She closed her eyes and shuddered. "I am sorry," she whispered.

"Sorry!"

"You will die and I will be responsible, when I thought only to save you," she moaned.

His broad chest rose and fell heavily as he registered her misery. Even now, she thought first of his safety, not her own. It was humbling. His big, six-fingered hands smoothed down the soft skin of her arms, tugging her closer. "I was too harsh," he confessed. "I have no fear of battle or death, but your welfare is another matter. I could not bear seeing you harmed."

"You could not?" Her great eyes opened into his, revealing secrets.

He groaned inwardly at the expression on her face. "You are a child, chasing dreams and adventure. I am an old warrior, scarred and bloodied. I am not fit for such as you."

"Old?"

He laughed bitterly. "In my own culture, yes. You see, the Rojok also used the DNA enhancements that have destroyed the original genome of your own people. We did not dare risk letting our enemies, the Cehn-Tahr, develop greater physical abilities than we had. I am the age of your Commander Dtimun, more or less." His eyes narrowed and he smiled. "While I doubt that you have seen more than seventy summers."

She cleared her throat.

One eye ridge lifted, for Rojoks had no eyebrows. "Less?"

She averted her eyes.

"Sixty?"

She hesitated, and then nodded. His hands released her. It was worse than he had thought. She truly was a child in her own culture. Barely a woman.

"So now you will not want to speak to me again. You think I am too young." Her lips tightened. Tears threatened. "You do not…want me."

His eyes closed. A wave of anguish washed over him. Want her! He would die to have her, and he could not admit it, not now. He felt a tingling in his mind and his eyes opened. Hers were pale blue, intense and... stunned.

He glared at her. "Unethical," he bit off.

She nodded. Then she walked right up against him and slid her arms around him, pressing close, holding on tight, with her soft cheek against the leather of his shirt. He hesitated, but only for an instant, before his arms closed around her fiercely. He recalled then his anguish when he found her at Ahkmau, racing across the galaxy to spare her the horrors of torture ordered by then-emperor Mangus Lo. He had been too late. She had been subjected to subsonics and her mind had been in full retreat. He had risked his career, his life, to bring Dtimun to her, to coax her back from certain death. It had been the happiest moment he could remember, when her soft, elegant eyes opened and looked at him.

"I know what you feel," she whispered at his chest. "You may try to hide it, but strong emotions are more difficult to conceal. And I am a telepath."

"You are never out of my thoughts," he whispered back. "But what you seek is not possible. Your father is Emperor of the Cehn-Tahr. I may command the Rojok fleet, but I am a soldier, a commoner. I have no royal status."

"It will not matter. My father has more respect for courage than social status."

He laughed shortly. "Not when the future of his daughter is in question."

"We can agree to disagree. At the moment, your safety is my greatest concern," she said.

He drew back. "And yours is mine. You should not have come."

She smiled tenderly. "I know."

He touched her cheek lightly and then laid his forehead against hers, in the Cehn-Tahr greeting between family members. "When we leave the shop, you will go back to your hotel and remain there, safe, until I can find a way to deal with the loss of your documents. Do you understand?"

"Yes." She sighed and pressed close. The world could end, now, and she would not notice.

MADELINE HAD ORDERED a tiny cup of the delicious imported Dacerian coffee and sipped it at the bar while she looked around at the traffic. Aliens on foot wandered from store to door. Some in one-person conveyances whizzed along the narrow streets at low speeds. Occasionally there was the sound of a flute as a robber was pursued by Benaski Port security forces. It was a busy, colorful marketplace. Madeline loved it.

When she finished her coffee, Sfilla was still arguing with the shopkeeper, her elegant hands waving in the air as she ridiculed the price he was charging for such a bit of mundane fabric. He, in turn, was arguing that his fabric was the finest sensor weave in the known galaxies and she was a peasant who knew nothing of quality merchandise.

Chuckling, Madeline got up and moved into the crowd. She paused at a shop of beautiful handmade veils, and was looking through them, when she heard a familiar voice.

Curious, she moved to the back of the shop. Now there were two voices, one male and thickly accented as he spoke Rojok, one feminine and soft, pleading. There was a long silence, and then the male walked out without looking anyplace except straight ahead.

She moved quickly past the shopkeeper, who was inviting an Altairian woman to try on one of the veils, and followed behind the Rojok, who was wearing a hooded robe. She recognized his carriage and his big booted feet more than his voice. It was Chacon!

He paused to speak to two Rojoks, dressed in the same black uniform as the one he wore under his robes. He pushed back the hood and his long, straight blond hair fell to the middle of his back. He ignored passersby as he gave what sounded like firm orders to them.

Madeline came up beside him and tugged at his arm.

He glared at her from slit eyes in a dusky face. "Go away," he said icily.

"I must speak with you," she said, wary of eavesdroppers.

"I have nothing to say to a female of the streets," he added, and turned away from her.

She kicked him in the leg.

He whirled, furious.

She opened her eyes wide. They were green. Even among Dacerian women with red hair, this eye color was unknown.

Chacon's eyes opened wide and he stared at her with dawning recognition.

"You wish to be entertained?" she said in imitation of a Dacerian woman's purring voice. "I make you good price."

"By all means," Chacon said with now-twinkling eyes. "If I am not too crippled to accommodate you," he added as he flexed the leg she'd kicked. He turned to his companions, who were grinning. "I will return soon."

They saluted him and moved away.

Chacon waited until they were out of sight before he turned back to Ruszel. Now his eyes registered the lump under her robes and he blinked. "Ruszel?" he asked under his breath. He scowled. "What are you doing here, like that?" he indicated her obvious pregnancy.

"Saving your butt, sir," she said. "You must come with me. I'm not here alone," she added meaningfully.

He caught his breath. "This is insane!" he blurted out.

"Oh, I do agree with that," she replied, trying to smile. The pain suddenly doubled her over and she was sick on the street. "No…!" she groaned. "Not…now!"

"Dtimun will kill me," he said under his breath. But he swung Madeline up in his powerful arms, just the same, when her sickness abated and started down the street with her. "Where are we going?"

"You're driving, sir, figuratively speaking—I'm just a passenger," she managed wanly. The nausea was almost unmanageable. "Sfilla is with me. She's at…the fabric shop, there."

Sfilla had just made her purchase and spotted Madeline being carried by a Rojok. She came rushing forward belligerently, with an odd, smooth grace that sat strangely on a female servant. Suddenly a silvery little knife flashed low in her hand, catching the glint of the neon lights.

"He's a friend!" Madeline said quickly, before Sfilla could act. Amazing, that Sfilla would risk attacking him for her. "Show him…where we're staying."

"A friend. He is a Rojok!"

"Yes. Do as I say. Quickly…!" Her voice broke off and Sfilla suddenly realized that she was in great pain.

Sfilla put the knife away, watching the Rojok warily. "We have a skimmer," she said. "It is here."

She led the tall Rojok to the skimmer and watched him put Madeline gently down on the small backseat. He climbed in the driver's seat, glaring when Sfilla tried to argue. Madeline groaned and Sfilla immediately gave in, telling Chacon the name of their hotel. He didn't spare the engine getting Madeline there.

Dtimun was studying a virtual computer readout when Chacon came in, with Madeline in his arms, flanked by a worried Sfilla.

"Chacon!" Dtimun burst out.

Sfilla's eyes were almost comically wide as she realized belatedly who their companion was.

"What happened to her?" Dtimun asked, too shocked to protest the Rojok touching his mate. He had just arrived back at the hotel, his search for the alien commander fruitless, only to have him walk in the door. It was ironic.

"Growth spurt, I imagine," he replied as he put her on the wide sofa. "We have officers who have mated with humans," he explained belatedly, grinning. "She has herbs to take for this, surely?"

Sfilla groaned. "I meant to obtain herbs from the market to replenish our stores! I did not have time!"

"Go back," Chacon said firmly. "Hurry."

"Yes!" She was gone with one last worried look at Madeline, who was groaning in pain.

"Does she have anything for pain?" Chacon asked Dtimun.

"In her wrist unit, but I do not know how to access

it," Dtimun said, kneeling beside Madeline to take her cold hand in his.

"And you are too emotionally involved to remove the pain," Chacon said solemnly. "I do not have the gift."

"But, I do," came a soft, melodious voice from the doorway. "What a good thing I followed you," she told Chacon.

CHAPTER SEVEN

PRINCESS LYCERIA PUSHED back the hood of her own cloak and walked gracefully into the room. She smiled secretly at Chacon and moved to Dtimun's side as he bent over Madeline.

Her smile faded when she saw the pain that tautened the human face. She knelt at the sofa. Her soft hand went to Madeline's cheek.

"The pain is a shadow," she said softly. "It moves behind your eyes. You cannot see it. You cannot feel it. The pain is a shadow. It passes in the darkness. It is gone."

Madeline gasped. It really was gone! She stared up at the beautiful Cehn-Tahr woman, fascinated. "Thank you. I will never get used to people being able to do that," she said.

Lyceria smiled. "It is a gift. Many have it," she added quickly when she saw wheels turning in Madeline's mind. "You know of us only through what textdiscs tell you, but there are many inconsistencies in such histories."

"I suppose so." She glanced from Chacon to Lyceria and smiled. "What a lucky thing that I insisted on going into the city today, and that Sfilla insisted on going with me." She glanced at Dtimun suspiciously. "Were you aware that she carries a knife?"

Chacon chuckled. "Of course she does. She is one of his government's finest assassins."

"Assassins?" Madeline burst out, sitting up in a jack-knife motion.

Dtimun gently pushed her back down. "She is not paid to assassinate you," he told her. "Only to protect you."

"Which she almost assassinated me in doing," Chacon murmured. He gave Madeline a speaking glance and bent to rub his shin. "After your mate crippled me," he told Dtimun.

"I did not," Madeline returned haughtily. "I had to get your attention somehow, sir, and you were doing your best to push me off."

"There must have been a less painful method, Ruszel."

"Is it my fault that I don't have social skills?" she asked the room at large. "What do I know about enticing a man, excuse me, a Rojok, for immoral purposes?"

"What was that?" Dtimun asked, staring at Chacon with cold, furious eyes.

"I never touched her!" Chacon argued. "Except to bring her here. I do not think Sfilla could have carried her, and it was dangerous to leave her lying in the street!"

"I would like to point out that if there's any fault, it was mine," Madeline said, exasperated, as she glared at Dtimun. "And would you mind explaining why you have a paid assassin pretending to be my servant woman?"

Dtimun grimaced, a very human expression. "The pregnancy makes you vulnerable to attack," he said through his teeth. "It would have been unwise to allow you out of my sight alone, especially here in this haven for thieves and murderers."

"He does have a point, Ruszel," Chacon said. He frowned. "You were at the point of death only a short time ago. How is that you and he—" he indicated Dtimun "—are here together in such a disguise?"

"A question I should also like answered," Princess Lyceria said worriedly. "You must be aware of the risk you take!"

"We have a…crewman," Dtimun said, choosing his words, "who has traveled in time. He came back, among other reasons, to find a means of saving your life," he told Chacon flatly. "He said that if you die, this timeline dies with you."

Chacon scoffed. "A seer," he said gruffly. "They are flawed."

"They are not," Princess Lyceria said firmly. "We have such a seer at Mahkmannah. It was she who saw Ruszel's rise to prominence among us, who predicted her emergence as a catalyst to change our world."

Chacon stared at her with eyes that quickly changed from mockery to frank affection. "Perhaps there are some who have the gift," he conceded. "But what danger could I possibly be in?" he added. "I have my bodyguard, including Lieumek who is the oldest and most trusted of my underlings. They never leave me. And Chan Ho," he added, "would not dare send assassins after me. I am far more popular with our people than he is. It would be political suicide!"

"That's why he plans to have you kidnapped, sir," Madeline said gently, "and sold into slavery. You would disappear. There would be no body, no certainty of death, but you would be removed and Chan Ho would build more ovens at Ahkmau."

"She speaks truth," Dtimun agreed. "Which brings us to our presence here." He gave Princess Lyceria a look that promised retribution. "Your family is frantic," he said coldly. "Your presence here only heightens the risk to Chacon."

"I had to warn him," Lyceria argued. "I tried sending messages, but I could not penetrate the nexus controls with flashes. I had no idea that any of you knew the true situation, which I learned from Captain—" she stopped at once "—from a soldier of my acquaintance."

"Rhemun," Dtimun said with a flash of brown anger. "I will have something to say to him when we return."

"If Edris Mallory hasn't killed him by then," Madeline said with pursed lips.

"Pardon me?" the princess asked.

"Mallory is Madeline's assistant," Dtimun explained with faint amusement. "She has taken a violent dislike to the captain of the *kehmatemer*, and he to her."

"There was a rumble before we left Memcache," Madeline agreed. "She threw a soup ladle at him, and he turned a pot of soup over her head."

The princess had to smother a laugh. So did Chacon.

"That does not sound like the captain," Lyceria commented.

"Who is supposed to be kidnapping me?" Chacon interrupted. "I have only my bodyguard with me here."

"Yes, but why did you come here?" Dtimun wanted to know.

Lyceria looked guilty. Chacon glanced at her and grimaced.

"I see," Dtimun murmured coolly.

"I had to warn him," Lyceria repeated defensively. "He saved our lives at *Ahkmau*."

"He's saved mine twice," Madeline replied quietly, with a glance at Chacon. "When Komak told us the danger of doing nothing, we thought the risk was worth our lives."

Lyceria had only just noticed the bulge under Madeline's robes. She caught her breath. "That cannot be what it looks like," she said hesitantly, with a truly frightened look at Dtimun. "The protocols…!"

Dtimun raised an eyebrow and bent to draw back, discreetly, the fabric from Madeline's collarbone, where the scar of bonding was noticeable.

"You have bonded?" Lyceria said, aghast. She went very still. "With…witnesses?"

Dtimun nodded. "Caneese performed the ceremony and the court physicians attended Madeline subsequently."

"So many people, to know such a dangerous secret," Lyceria groaned.

"Caneese will make certain that the secret is kept," Dtimun said. "You must also swear not to reveal it. Madeline's pregnancy is the only protection we will have while we search for the assassin."

"Yes, and it is a wise disguise," Lyceria agreed, "but what about afterward?" she asked with real and evident concern for both of them.

Madeline's thoughts were laid bare. She was too unsettled to block them.

Lyceria gasped. She stared at Madeline with horror. "You would regress the child?" she exclaimed. "But it is not possible!"

Madeline was very calm. "It's a simple procedure,"

she said gently. "He'll be absorbed back into the tissues of my body."

"The part of him that is you, will be," Lyceria corrected, her lovely eyes almost wincing. "But the part that is Cehn-Tahr, which is sentient, cannot be absorbed. It would have to be surgically removed, and the pain…!"

Madeline had not, until that moment, realized the flaw in her own argument. The child had two strands of DNA: Dtimun's and her own. Alien DNA, unlike human, could never be absorbed back into her body. And if the child was truly sentient even at this early stage, it would be agony.… She ground her teeth together.

Dtimun said nothing. But he looked at Lyceria with an opaque blue stare, which she answered with one of her own.

Madeline frowned at what seemed like a staring contest. But she knew it was something more.

Chacon glanced at Madeline and sighed. "They converse in a manner which we cannot understand," he said. "Let us hope they are not plotting something unspeakable."

After a minute, the two Cehn-Tahr stopped communicating. Dtimun's eyes were laughing as he looked at Madeline. So were Lyceria's.

Madeline glanced at Sfilla, who had just entered the room. "Did you hear any of that?" she asked with a pointed glare. "Assassins should be able to read minds as well as lips. And thank you very much for offering to let me teach you hand-to-hand. You're probably a master trainer!"

Sfilla grinned. "I am. I am skilled in all martial arts,

including the Kahn-Bo, in which I have only one or two superiors. I, too, learned my craft as a child."

Madeline shook her head. "I never suspected."

"You are only vulnerable while you carry the child," Sfilla said gently. "I am useful during this time. Do not resent my presence."

"I wasn't resenting it," Madeline assured her. She laughed. "It will give us more to talk about when we don't have anything else to do." She glanced at Chacon. "But now that we've found you, sir, it's still a question of rooting out your potential kidnappers and preventing them from doing their job."

"I agree," Dtimun said. "Both of you must move into this hotel. In separate rooms," he added with a pointed glance at Lyceria, who actually blushed.

"The princess has nothing to fear from me in that regard," Chacon assured Dtimun stiffly. "I know the law."

"So does he, but that doesn't stop him from breaking it," Madeline piped in.

Dtimun shot her a hot glare. "You will refrain from speaking of me in such a manner."

"Oh, get real," she muttered back. "What are you going to do, sir, put me on report and stick me in the brig?" She looked around. "Where are you going to find a brig on Benaski Port?"

Dtimun's lips made a thin line. "You can be confined to your room. There are master locks!"

"And I can break out of windows!" she shot back with glittering green eyes.

Lyceria, fascinated and amused, moved between them. "There is the matter of the kidnapping?" she reminded them.

Madeline shifted on the sofa, still glowering at Dtimun, who was glaring at her. But they stopped arguing.

All at once, Madeline gasped and touched her stomach. The child was not only moving, he was reproving her for fighting with his father. She stared at Dtimun, uncertain whether she should reveal the fact that she could communicate with the child in her womb.

He moved closer, knelt and placed his hand on her swollen stomach. He smiled. Then he laughed. He glanced at Chacon and Lyceria. "He does not like it when his parents argue."

"He speaks to you?" Lyceria asked, fascinated.

Dtimun nodded. He looked up at Madeline. She laughed.

"Human babies don't do this," Madeline tried to explain. Then she thought of the regression and anguish overcame her.

Dtimun touched his forehead to hers. "You must not think of these things. You must concentrate on why we are here. The rest will be sorted out in the future. You must trust me, as you always have."

She didn't understand what he meant, but she didn't argue. Her hand came up and smoothed the hair at his temple. It did, she thought, feel so much like thick fur....

He pulled back, still smiling.

CHACON HAD MANY contacts among the underworld figures who inhabited Benaski Port. He took Dtimun with him to try to dig information out of them about his potential kidnapping. But even the friendliest of them knew nothing specific. There were rumors. But nothing more could be ascertained.

"This is frustrating," Dtimun muttered when they returned to the hotel.

Chacon sighed. "I still find it difficult to believe that Chan Ho would resort to such a foolish act."

"I can see his point of view," the other alien remarked. "He would not dare have you killed. He would be immediately suspect, as the two of you have argued political viewpoints too often."

"It would be convenient for him if I vanished," Chacon muttered. "He would rebuild Ahkmau and return the terror policies of Mangus Lo which I opposed for so many years."

"Your race's political leaders leave much to be desired," Dtimun said curtly.

Chacon chuckled. "I will not return the accusation. Your government has a stability which is quite envied in the three galaxies."

"We can credit the emperor with that stability," he mused. "Our provincial governors are capable and incorruptible, as well."

"Your emperor has held power for many years. What will happen when he steps down?" Chacon wondered aloud. "He has no heir."

Dtimun averted his eyes. "The Clan Alamantimichar is not without candidates."

"Yes, but it will take a strong hand to rule an empire."

Dtimun nodded. "The emperor has ruled for centuries. Considering his life span, I think it unlikely that he will need to abdicate in favor of an heir." He said. "It is amusing to consider him in a retirement ward."

"That will never happen," Chacon laughed.

"I agree." Dtimun sobered. "We still have no clue as to your potential kidnappers. This is frustrating."

Lyceria walked into the room and smiled at the two males. Sfilla was right behind her. "Have you found out something?" Lyceria asked.

Chacon smiled at her. "You can read minds," Chacon replied. "Perhaps if we walk through the bazaar and you focus your attention on the shops…?"

Lyceria returned the smile. "It is not so easy to single out one individual's thoughts from those of a crowd. Even for me."

Chacon sighed. "I could stand in the pavilion in the center of the city and wait for developments."

Dtimun shook his head. "Unwise."

"I do not like a threat hanging over my head." His slitted eyes narrowed even more. "I will have Lieumek activate his spy network and see if he can determine a suspect."

"Can you think of an agent who would accept such an assignment?"

Chacon frowned, deep in thought. "I know the head of our intelligence services. He and my family are linked through marriage. I might contact him."

"Do it covertly and do not tell him where you are," the other advised quietly.

Chacon laughed. "He can be trusted."

"No one can be trusted in such circumstances," Dtimun said curtly.

"Very well. But you are wrong about him."

"We shall see."

"If you please," Sfilla interrupted, "let me use my sources before you commit to such an action." Her expression was open, concerned.

Chacon sighed. He looked at Dtimun, who nodded. "Very well. I will wait to contact him. For the moment."

"I will get to work at once," Sfilla said. She even smiled.

"She has a kind smile," Chacon mused. "I imagine it would remain while she was slitting my throat."

"She is not sanctioned to murder you," Dtimun chuckled.

"For which, I thank providence," the alien commander said.

LYCERIA WALKED OUT onto the balcony that overlooked the city, where Chacon stood quietly contemplating the neon lights that seemed to stretch forever toward the black horizon.

He turned at her approach. "You cannot sleep, either," he mused.

She shrugged, smiling. "I do not sleep well in strange places."

He leaned back against the balcony and studied her with eyes that appreciated her long, flowing black hair, the way the soft blue robes clung to her slender figure. She was quite beautiful.

She was also admiring him. He was tall and powerfully built. In his close fitting, black military uniform, he seemed larger than life. He was regal, in his way, a respected and envied commander whose strategies, like Dtimun's, were taught in many cadet academies in the three galaxies.

"We are unalike," Chacon said abruptly as he studied her. "Much as Dtimun and Madeline."

She smiled. "Their differences are far greater. Our species are both Cularian."

He nodded. "It is a shame, about their child," he remarked quietly. "I sense that they both want it very much." He turned away. "I feel responsible. They took a great risk to save me."

"One they were quite willing to take," she replied. "And there are things we are not permitted to know," she added in a faintly amused tone.

He glanced at her with mischievous eyes. "You can read minds," he said suggestively.

She nodded. "A great gift. But I will not trespass in Commander Dtimun's thoughts to learn them. Telepathy can be abused."

"Not by you, my lady," he replied gently.

She stiffened. "Please do not address me so," she pleaded. "I am not your superior."

"The daughter of an emperor," he began.

She reached up and put her soft fingers against his hard, chiseled mouth. "A female," she whispered. "Just a female."

His whole body tautened at her touch. Since his first glimpse of her, on Enmehkmehk, his home planet, he had been consumed by his feelings for her. They seemed to intensify over the years. It had touched and flattered him that she returned them. In defiance of protocol and law, they had maintained contact throughout the war, covertly, managing to avoid detection even by the *kehmatemer*.

"You are wondering how I escaped the scrutiny of the *kehmatemer* to come here," she teased. She stepped closer. "You are also thinking that I am very desirable, and you wish I were not the child of an emperor."

"Stop," he muttered, catching the hand that was

smoothing over his dusky face. "You will tempt me into indiscretion, with witnesses in the next room."

She laughed, the sound of silver bells in the darkness. "They are too busy working on holographic weapon prototypes to notice us. Her competence as a military officer still fascinates me."

He laughed, too. "Ruszel is unique," he mused. "He will fight to keep her, I think."

She traced a pattern on the black fabric that covered his broad chest. "Indeed he will." She stared at his chest instead of his face. "As you fought your government, your emperor, to save my life at Ahkmau."

He recalled those early days with anger. Mangus Lo, the Rojok tyrant leader, had sent Lyceria to Ahkmau with instructions to torture her to death. When he knew her fate, Chacon took his personal bodyguard and decimated Mangus Lo's personal guard to save her. In the process, he had saved Dtimun and Ruszel and the Holconcom.

"Madeline was willing to sacrifice her life, to save Dtimun's," Lyceria murmured. "She almost died. Her feelings for him are intense."

"I think his are equally intense, for her," he replied. "A shame that your government will put him to death if her condition becomes known."

Lyceria pursed her lips. "Our emperor is quite fascinated by Ruszel. I do not think he would permit her to be harmed."

He cocked his head. "How does he know her?"

"The *kehmatemer* made her acquaintance on Ondar, under unusual circumstances. They talk about her constantly, especially Captain Rhemun, who leads the *kehmatemer*." She laughed. "Rhemun's heart is soft for her, which causes a hot and noticeable reaction on the part of the Holconcom commander."

"Cehn-Tahr mating behaviors are quite different from those of my race. Ours are less brutal," he pointed out.

Her eyes met his. "And I am like the rest of my race, intensely strong and resilient," she said. "Ruszel had to be genetically modified to breed with my...with Dti-mun," she corrected quickly. "Otherwise, she would certainly have died."

He frowned. "These genetic modifications are disturbing, even to my race. I wish that we had not tampered with our genome."

"Yes, I feel the same. An attempt to improve our race has caused great pain and suffering to generations of us." She stared at him with gentle eyes. "At least you would not require genetic modification to breed with me," she said boldly, and laughed at his expression.

He did not smile. He looked away. "You are the child of an emperor. I am a soldier. One of my antecedents was a minor royal, but I have no claim to the aristocracy... Why are you laughing?" he snapped, offended.

She moved closer and placed both hands over his chest. She could feel the hard, heavy beat of his heart in anger. "I mean no offense," she said softly. "But you are too modest about your standing in your society. You are the most famous Rojok military leader in the history of the three galaxies. Your strategies are studied by cadets of every race, even those who are enemies of your people. You are respected, even admired, by leaders of opposing armies. Your reputation for even-handedness and fairness in battle is far-reaching." She looked him in the eye. "You are the equivalent of Rojok royalty, even if you do not realize it. And my father is one of those who has great respect for you."

"Your father?" he asked, surprised.

She nodded. She smiled. "You risked your life to go to Akaashe to bargain with the Nagaashe for Madeline's release, as a negotiator. The emperor was quite impressed."

"Ruszel is human, not Cehn-Tahr," he began.

"Ruszel is being given Cehn-Tahr citizenship and a high military rank," she said surprisingly. "She made possible a treaty with the Nagaashe, which our greatest negotiators have never managed to obtain. This is why your part in her rescue has gained the emperor's favor." She lowered her eyes to his chest. "I think he would not object if you wished to bond with me. Once the war is ended," she added sadly. "Whenever that may be."

He was struck dumb by the remarks. He had not realized that the emperor even knew of him, except through battle vids. There had been no real contact between them except for a modified vidlink which distorted both the voice and the features of the imperial leader when Tnurat had asked him to go to Akaashe to negotiate for the release of Ruszel and her crew.

She looked up again. She felt very insecure, despite her assurance of his affection. "That is, if you wished to bond with me, one day."

He felt her vulnerability, and smiled with pure affection. He touched her cheek with his fingertips and bent to press his forehead against hers. "There is nothing I wish more," he whispered. "Except that I could wish you were only an aristocrat and not an emperor's child. I am not ambitious of political power, but it would be intimated that power prompted my interest in you."

She slid her arms around him, shyly, and pressed close. "Those who know you would not think that, and the opinion of enemies is never important."

He laughed. He held her close and rocked her against him. He laid his cheek against her dark hair and closed his eyes, drinking in the floral fragrance that clung to her body.

"I envy Madeline," she said softly. "It must be poignant, to carry the child of a beloved mate."

"Yes." He let out a strained breath. "I should like, very much, to breed with you," he whispered in her ear.

She caught her breath and shivered, just a little. The mating cycle in females was less intense than in Cehn-Tahr males, and usually only initiated by mating itself. But she felt an intense longing all the same. She felt needs that she had never contemplated in her young life when Chacon held her.

His big hands smoothed down her back, bringing her even closer. A soft groan passed his lips.

She rubbed her head against his chest and made a low, rumbling sound, deep in her throat.

He buried his face in her throat, his lips rough against the soft flesh. He was consumed with fevers, with aching needs. He bent and lifted her off the floor. His eyes, as they met hers, were flaming.

"Put her down," Dtimun said calmly, from the doorway.

Chacon and Lyceria looked at him blankly, frozen in the moment.

"Put her down," Dtimun repeated firmly, although his eyes were green with fond amusement. "This is not the time."

Chacon looked at the submissive female in his arms and groaned.

Lyceria peered at Dtimun from calming features, and a wry little smile touched her lips. "Could you be persuaded to leave the hotel for a few days?" she asked amusedly.

He glowered at her. "The emperor would put my head on a stick and have vids made of it," he replied.

She laughed out loud, the idea was so preposterous.

Chacon set her back on her feet, with an amused, but strained, expression. "Since he will not leave, we must behave with decorum," he sighed.

"There must be a bonding," Dtimun reminded them. "And we are at war."

They both grimaced.

"That being said, I do understand," he added gently.

"I suppose you do," Lyceria agreed.

Chacon chuckled. "Perhaps we should remain in company, for the time being," he told Lyceria with a new and delighted knowledge of her. "We would not want to risk Dtimun's head."

Lyceria studied him with amusement. "No. Although I very much doubt his assessment of the consequences," she teased.

He gave her a cold, meaningful look, and she cleared her throat.

"There are news vids about the latest skirmish between your troops and ours," Dtimun told Chacon with dancing green eyes.

Chacon burst out laughing. "I trust my troops are winning?" he taunted.

"Against the vanguard of the Cehn-Tahr?" Dtimun chuckled. "Amusing."

Chacon took Lyceria's hand closely in his, and enjoyed her soft flush. "Perhaps there are better programs to view," he commented, glancing past Dtimun at Madeline, who was talking to Sfilla in the suite's living room beyond the balcony. "I think your mate will not like your choice of programs."

Dtimun glanced at Madeline with warm, hungry eyes. "Then a nature special about the galots might suffice to amuse her," he commented. He laughed. "As usual, the researchers have gained very little information on the species. The vid is full of fabrications."

"That is because the galots consume research teams who land on their home planet," Lyceria murmured.

Dtimun motioned them into the room and turned on the nature vid feed. He was still smiling when Madeline joined them.

She sat down next to Dtimun on the wide chaise and gaped at the screen. There was a depiction of a galot screaming in some odd cat howls which, the show's host explained, was how the great cats conversed with one another.

She looked up at Dtimun with her eyebrows almost meeting her hairline. "Has this guy ever actually seen a galot, you think?" she asked.

He chuckled. "I was wondering the same thing."

Chacon, who had no familiarity with the species, was puzzled. "Wakken on our planet communicate in such a fashion," he commented, naming a sort of giant wolf.

"Galots are, shall we say, somewhat more sophisticated in their forms of communication," Madeline told him.

"Yes, they communicate with researchers by eating

them," Lyceria told Chacon with evident glee. "Which is why this vid flasher is fabricating his conclusions."

Dtimun cocked his head and studied the human flash journalist. He shook his head. "They would not consume this one."

"No?" Madeline asked, fascinated. "Why not?"

"Because he is Terravegan," Lyceria commented.

Madeline and Chacon exchanged curious glances.

"He is a vegetarian, as most of the non-military humans are," Dtimun told them, smiling. "No galot will eat a human who consumes only vegetation. He would consider the taste offensive."

"Well, I know one thing," Madeline commented. "If I ever set foot in the primary Eridanus planetary system, I'm becoming a vegan before I get off the ship!"

And they all laughed.

CHAPTER EIGHT

BETWEEN THEM, DTIMUN and Chacon had gone through every contact they had, trying to locate the operatives that Chan Ho had sent after Chacon. There were many rumors, but no facts. They could only learn that the kidnapping was to take place soon, and that the operatives were already in place.

Madeline had one contact of her own, and she led the two alien commanders to a shady arms dealer in the back room of a gambling shop. But the contact knew nothing. He did, however, seem to notice the direction they took when they left him. And he accessed a private vid channel shortly thereafter.

"It's so frustrating," Madeline muttered as they walked. "Somebody in Benaski Port must know something they could tell us."

"Such information comes at a price," Chacon mused. "But I agree, we cannot even find someone to bribe for intel."

"Perhaps your new friend has a contact," Dtimun said suddenly, turning to Madeline. "He knows people here quite well."

"You mean Mardol?" Madeline asked. She pursed her lips. "That's not a bad idea. We could ask him."

They took a shuttle to the hotel district, but there was, of all things, a traffic jam. They exited the shuttle and anticipated a long walk to the hotel. Madeline's expression was weary.

"There is a shortcut to your hotel across this bridge," Chacon said, anticipating Dtimun's reluctance to let Madeline walk so far in her rapidly deteriorating condition. The pregnancy was advancing quickly, and the pain and fatigue were greatly intensified. She couldn't hide it.

Dtimun frowned. "It might be unwise to move along such an isolated path."

"It might be more unwise to let your mate walk so far here," Chacon said, indicating Madeline's strained face.

"I can carry her," Dtimun said easily.

Madeline glared up at him. "I can walk," she said shortly. "I'm not an invalid. I'm just pregnant."

"Very pregnant," Dtimun murmured with soft golden eyes. He felt great pride in her condition, and the way she carried herself.

She saw that. It fascinated her. She managed a grin. "The sky route it is, then. Is there an accelerator up there?"

"I believe so," Chacon said. "If it works."

So many things in Benaski Port that were supposed to work, didn't, Madeline thought amusedly. But perhaps this one was. The weather was being badly managed. The heat of the asteroid in its dome was stifling. She felt it more because of her condition.

They took a lifter up to the top of the building and found, to their dismay, that the accelerator pad was, indeed, out of order.

"It is still closer to go this way than to attempt the path through the traffic and crowds below," Chacon said.

"I agree," Dtimun seconded. He glanced at Madeline with some concern.

"Lay on, McDuff," she taunted. "I'm perfectly fit, I am."

"McDuff?" Chacon asked, frowning.

"A human idiom," Dtimun said with an affectionate glance at Madeline. "It means…!"

He broke off as an explosion went off just in front of them as they walked across a rooftop that was empty except for a square weather unit barely adequate to provide cover to all three of them.

With lightning reflexes, Dtimun picked Madeline up and ran to the only cover available, closely followed by Chacon.

"A sniper!" Madeline exclaimed breathlessly when they were behind the unit. "That was an explosive sensor pack, and it's a miracle he misjudged the distance. I'll bet he's using an emerillium psyoscillilator to program it. Those things are outdated, but some assassins still swear by them."

Before Chacon could question her intimate knowledge of such a detail, another round exploded on the other side of the unit.

Of all the bad luck, she muttered to herself. It was unbelievable that three seasoned warriors could be caught out in the open with only a small block weather control unit between them and a determined sniper. It would not be possible to reach the window of the hotel before they were picked off. Even a champion sprinter would not survive the open area with the Rojoks' perfected targeting tech.

Madeline muttered under her breath. The growth

spurt was painful and a little frightening, but being un-
armed was worse. "If we only had a gun," she grumbled.

"I do have a *chasat*," Chacon mused. "However, it
would do us little good against a distant sniping em-
placement."

"Indeed," Dtimun agreed, his concerned gaze covertly on Madeline.

She remembered something all at once. She turned to
the commander. "Can you contact Lyceria mentally?"

"Of course," he replied. "Why?"

"I need you to tell her to get Sfilla to go to Mardol
and ask to borrow his sniper kit."

His eyes smiled. "I begin to understand the old fellow's assessment of your battle skills," he said. He
closed his eyes for a few seconds, opened them and
nodded. "Lyceria is sending Sfilla now to ask Mardol
for the sniper kit. She will bring the sniper kit to the
window," he said after a minute.

"A sniper kit?" Chacon asked. "I must tell you, I have
no experience with it."

"Nor do I," Dtimun returned.

"Then of what use is it?"

"Wait and see."

Only a few minutes passed until Sfilla appeared at
the window with old Mardol, who was carrying the
heavy weapon case. He peered out the window and argued with her.

Dtimun closed his eyes. Sfilla took the case from the
old warrior and balanced it on the windowsill. Dtimun
nodded toward it, and the case suddenly sped down to
the roof and moved like a snake across the distance
until he had it in hand...

"I'd love to be able to do that," Madeline mused.

She turned to the case, flipped it open and quickly assembled the sniper rifle. "Sir, may I borrow the power pack from your *chasat?*" she asked Chacon when she had it assembled.

He removed the power pack and handed it to her, his eyebrow ridges arching when she snapped it home in the power core compartment. "You are familiar with the weapon," he concluded.

She grinned. "When I was eight years old, I was placed in a forward commando unit as a sniper. I was undefeated in competition within my entire division."

She tried to lift the rifle and suddenly felt her strength diminish as another growth spurt tautened her whole body.

"You can balance it on my shoulder," Dtimun offered.

She shook her head, fighting to breathe. "It wouldn't work, sir," she said respectfully. "It has to be a stationary support. Something that won't breathe," she added mischievously.

"She carries your child and still addresses you as 'sir'?" Chacon commented.

"A problem which I have labored unsuccessfully to resolve," Dtimun replied with a wry glance at Madeline.

He hit the preformed stone structure with his fist, and sent the material flying. He had made an indentation in it which would accommodate the underbelly of the gun. "Will this do?" he asked Madeline.

She nodded. "If you can lift it into place for me..."

He did. She got under it, breathing more freely now. She activated the virtual targeting scope and peered through it. On the roof, staring toward their position, were three humanoids. Two were Dacerian. The other...

She grimaced. "Sir," she said to Chacon, "one of the people targeting us is a Rojok. He's wearing the patch of your intelligence services."

"Describe him," Chacon replied.

"Tall, thin, a scar running down his face beside his nose…"

"Garathor," he said heavily. "Second-in-command of my personal spy service," he added coldly. "One of my most trusted comrades. No wonder Chan Ho knew where to find me."

Madeline hesitated.

He glanced at Madeline and noted her reluctance to fire. "We have no choice, Ruszel," Chacon said. "If we want to live."

She nodded. "Sorry, sir." She turned back to her targets, adjusted for elevation and atmosphere, and suddenly sent three bursts toward the distant snipers. She didn't even look. She turned away and indicated to Dtimun that he could remove the rifle.

Curious, he looked through the scope. All three snipers were on the floor of the opposing building. "Amazing," he said quietly.

"We all have skills," Madeline said quietly. "This is mine. But after a few years, it begins to kill the spirit."

"As most combat does," Chacon replied. "Thank you, Ruszel."

"You've saved my life several times, sir," she replied.

"And you have saved mine," Dtimun added to her, placing the heavy gun on the floor. He met her eyes with a shimmering green in his own. "Yes, I have not forgotten the scope of your accomplishment at Ahkmau, having been reminded of it daily for almost three years."

She grinned. "Here. I'll put it away."

She disassembled the rifle, using the cleaning material to make sure it was properly wiped free of chemicals before she put it back in the case. She handed the *chasat* power pack back to Chacon. They stood up. Dtimun carried the case for her.

Old Mardol was standing at the window with his eyes wide. "You used the sniper rifle!" he exclaimed to Madeline.

"Yes," she said, smiling. "Thank you for lending it to us. We were pinned down by sniper fire."

"You removed the threat?" he asked.

"Three threats."

"And only three shots," he replied, fascinated. "Amazing!" He stared at her. "You have been in the military."

She nodded. "In my youth," she added quickly. "I'm glad I haven't forgotten my old skills. They came in handy today."

"We must talk again," he said. "You can tell me some of your battle stories." He grinned.

Dtimun and Chacon were not smiling.

"The wounds will be examined and traced to this weapon," Dtimun told the old man, referencing nanotech that could pinpoint a weapon from trace evidence in seconds and locate its whereabouts. He turned to Sfilla and gave her instructions in Cehn-Tahr. She nodded and ran away. He turned back to the old soldier. "Pack what you need to carry. Sfilla is arranging passage to Memcache for you."

"But…but," the old man sputtered, "I am a wanted man…!"

"Not after today," Dtimun assured him. "You will

go to Mahkmannah, to our religious retreat. You will be safe."

Mardol searched for the right words. He couldn't find them. His eyes misted.

Dtimun put a hand on his shoulder, and his eyes went that odd opaque blue that indicated mind touching. "You were falsely accused and the only witness who could clear you is dead. I understand. However, you will find peace and safety at the religious retreat. You may stay there forever without fear of persecution. We owe you our lives. It will not be forgotten."

Mardol swallowed the lump in his throat. "I...have not been safe for two decades."

"Now, you will be. Pack quickly. Sfilla will escort you to the ship."

The old man paused, made a virtual note and handed it to Dtimun. "This is a man I know, who can give you information about any covert dealings here in Benaski Port. He will trust you, because I have told him to."

"We are in your debt," Chacon told him.

Mardol's old eyes narrowed on the three. "A strange combination. A Rojok, a Cehn-Tahr and a human." He smiled. "I hope someday I may know who you are."

"Sooner than you think, perhaps," Dtimun said. "Go on. It will not take our adversaries long to discover you."

Mardol nodded and turned down the hall with the sniper kit held in one big hand.

"They'll be after us again, too," Madeline pointed out as she followed the tall males down the hall. "And we're no closer to discovering our companion's would-be kidnappers."

Dtimun scanned the virtual note Mardol had give him. "Yes, but I think we have a contact who might.

Let us find him." He glanced at Chacon. "And considering the circumstances, I think it would be wise if you go back to the hotel and remain there. You should not be seen with us. If you are recognized, our true identities will be immediately uncovered and our mission will fail."

Chacon grimaced. "I concur, but reluctantly. I do not like the chances you take on my behalf, especially with Ruszel in such a condition."

"I'm quite lethal even in this condition, sir, and I want a future into which we can all survive and grow old," she retorted.

"As do we all," Dtimun said. "We will return shortly."

"If you do not," Chacon replied, "your finest assassin and I will come to search for you."

Dtimun smiled. "She has become fond of you. But do not mention this in front of her."

Chacon placed his hand over his heart, grinned and left them.

THE SHADY CHARACTER Mardol sent them to was a smuggler, an outcast human who deplored the totalitarian government of Terravega and became a wanderer, with no credentials. He was barred from legal transactions in the human colonies because of his lack of citizenship and the implanted DNA ID which all Terravegans were equipped with at birth. So he went underground as a young man and established a solid business transporting illegal goods from one colony to another. Most of his transactions dealt in weapons and foodstuffs. He was well-known in Benaski Port. And other places, some even more covert. Just occasionally, he was hired as an independent contractor to transport essential supplies to war-torn human colonies deep behind enemy lines.

His name was Percival Blount, but friends and enemies alike called him Patch. He had long black hair, which he wore in a ponytail, and one blue eye. The other eye, lost long ago in a knife fight, was covered by a black patch; hence the nickname. He had a straightforward manner and a ragged dignity that sat oddly on a pirate.

He shook hands with Dtimun and Madeline and offered them refreshment in his private cabin aboard the aging but serviceable space vessel he called home.

"She's old," he said with affection, looking around the metal-faced compartment. "But I've never had cause to regret her purchase."

"You call your ship a she?" Madeline, raised in a unisex environment, asked curiously.

"Yes, I do," he replied. He studied her with some amusement and added, "Lieutenant Commander Madeline Ruszel," he murmured with a grin at her surprise and consternation. "Or should I say, Dr. Ruszel?"

She hesitated, uncertain what to say.

"I have spies everywhere," he said, as he poured ancient brandy into a snifter. He offered the bottle, but both his visitors refused. "It amazes me, to see a human female pregnant with a Cehn-Tahr child," he continued. "It must be a Cehn-Tahr child, or you'd never have made it through what passes for customs here. We employ psy-techs to scan every visitor."

Madeline understood, then, why Komak had insisted that the pregnancy had been mandatory for the mission. Neither Madeline nor Dtimun had known that psy-techs did scans of so-called fugitives from justice here.

It wasn't publicized. But Patch still hadn't mentioned Dtimun's identity. The Holconcom never permitted publication of vids about its crew, or its commander. Dtimun's face was not known outside the unit.

Patch pursed his lip and studied Dtimun quietly. "You're an aristocrat, we figured that out. But we don't know from which Clan. Don't worry, I won't pry," he added when the alien's eyes darkened with a threat. "If either of your governments find out about that child, you'll both have a life span of less than one solar day. You know that already, I'm sure."

"Why do you think we're here?" Madeline asked with black humor.

"I hope you fare well," Patch said gently. "It's not an easy pregnancy. We had a human female pregnant by a Rojok a few years ago. Tragic story...they only wanted to live together here without complications. They were safe, but she died two months into the pregnancy." He shook his head while Madeline paled. Rojoks, like Cehn-Tahr, were Cularian humanoids.

"And Rojok babies are even smaller than Cehn-Tahr, who grow at an accelerated rate," Patch continued. "I studied medicine in my younger days," he added, surprising them. His jaw set. "I thought I could get around the clone issue. But I couldn't. I was required to grow and use human clones for replacement organs for high Terravegan officials. I refused." He shrugged. "So I don't practice medicine anymore. That knowledge comes in handy here, though," he added. "So if you go into labor, Doctor, you're welcome to send for me, and I'll come, wherever you are."

Madeline was honestly touched. "Thank you," she said. "I'm sorry for your experience."

He shrugged. "Life happens. What can I do for the two of you?" he added. "If Mardol sent you here, you need information. Right?"

She nodded. "We're looking for an assassin."

His eyebrows rose. "In Benaski Port? Good luck. Every third humanoid here deals in covert death," he added.

She grimaced. "That's probably true, but we're looking for a particular one. He's been sent to kidnap the Rojok Field Marshal, Chacon."

Now the one eye widened with shock. "You're human. He—" he indicated Dtimun with a nod "—is Cehn-Tahr. In case neither of you noticed," he added with amused sarcasm, "both your governments are at war with the Rojok Dynasty."

"Chacon saved our lives," Dtimun replied quietly. "We are in his debt. We know of a plot to kidnap him and sell him into slavery, to remove his influence from Chan Ho's government and allow a return to the terror policies of Mangus Lo."

Patch sat up straighter. "Bad news," he said. "Very bad news. I've done business with Chacon's under-lieutenant, Lieumek, in the past. In fact, Lieumek is involved with a Dacerian woman who comes here to shop." He sighed. "If Chacon disappears, I lose a lucrative business myself." His eyes narrowed. "Do you have any idea who the would-be kidnappers are?"

They both shook their heads.

"We know only that an attempt has been planned for some weeks," Dtimun told him.

Patch sipped brandy. His one eye narrowed. "There are a couple of people who've been inquiring about Rojok troop movements lately. I'll send one of my agents into the bazaar to ask questions. When I know something, I'll contact you. You're staying at a hotel outside the port, aren't you?"

."Yes," Madeline said, and named it.

He shook his head. "Must be nice," he sighed. "My digs are little more than a hut compared to the accommodations there. But one day I'll retire from piracy and become respectable." He leaned forward. "The *Freespirit* offered me work. I may take them up on it in future. Wouldn't that confound my enemies here?" he added with a laugh. He frowned. "Where is Mardol? His life is worth pocket change after he loaned you that sniper kit," he added, staring at Madeline. "Nice work, by the way. I wish you worked for me."

She laughed. "Do you know everything?"

He nodded.

"Mardol is already in a safe place," Dtimun said, without volunteering more information. "He saved our lives."

"Yours and an unknown Rojok's," Patch added.

"I'm sure you have some idea who the unknown Rojok was," Madeline said with a grin.

He nodded again. His one blue eye twinkled. "It didn't matter at the time where he went. We know what goes on here, but we don't pry. Hell, we've all got something to hide or we wouldn't be here in the first place!"

Madeline leaned forward. "Just FYI, I've been in a lot worse places."

He smiled. "I know. That information, about how the Morcai Battalion was formed, is pretty much public information."

"It is," Madeline agreed, "but some things we keep to ourselves."

"Yes, like your interesting condition and your relationship with a Cehn-Tahr aristocrat." He shook his head. "There isn't one case on record of a Cehn-Tahr mating with a human. Your child, if you survive the pregnancy—sorry—will be unique in the three galaxies."

Madeline's hand went protectively to her belly and she tried not to think of the future.

Dtimun stood and helped her up, his eyes affectionate. "You are tired," he said gently. "We must go." He glanced at Patch. "We will be in your debt for any information you can find out for us."

"Yes. In my debt," he added with a slow grin. "And one day I may call on you for help, financial or otherwise."

"You may, indeed," Dtimun replied, smiling. "And I will help, if I can."

Patch nodded respectfully. "There are herbs that can help retard the growth spurts of the child," he told Madeline. "We've had at least one successful pregnancy with a human mother and a Rojok father. They're not too different from the Cehn-Tahr."

They were very different, and there were genetic anomalies like the enhanced strength of Dtimun and his Clan. But he said nothing.

"I'll be in touch," Patch said as he saw them off.

MADELINE WAS DISTURBED about what Patch had told them, about the one human woman's fatal pregnancy. Since she was unaware of any medical precedents concerning human-Cularian offspring, the news was surprising.

"We don't have contact with the Rojoks, as a rule,"

she told Dtimun, "so we don't have much information about their efforts to breed with other races."

"The human female who died certainly had to conceal her pregnancy from Terravegan authorities and thereby limit her access to physicians," he said gently, stopping to turn to her and smooth her hair with affection. "It is not an immediate concern, either."

"No, of course not." But she was worried, all the same, more for the child than for herself. But why, she asked herself, when she wouldn't even get to bear her child…!

He pulled her into his arms, despite the public place, and held her. "No more brooding," he whispered. "You must trust me."

She held on tight, biting her lip to stop the tears. "I didn't expect to want him," she whispered.

His arms tightened. "Neither did I."

She managed a laugh and looked up with her heart in her eyes. "Couldn't we run away to the Rim? I'm certain that a doctor could find work up there, and you're peerless as a pilot." She said it in jest, but she was partially serious.

He lifted his head and smiled tenderly. "You have allies of whom you are unaware. I cannot say more, except to tell you once more that you must trust me."

"I always have," she said simply.

He traced her mouth and unexpectedly bent and pressed his own against it, very softly. "The future is not as dark as you anticipate."

She laughed. Her green eyes sparkled. He seemed to be optimistic. Could they have a future together, when it seemed impossible?

"Do not anticipate tomorrow," he whispered.

She made a face. "I'll try, sir."

He sighed. "Madeline…"

She made a stab at pronouncing his name, only the second time she'd ever used it. She flushed a little, remembering the first.

He laughed, delighted. "That is the formal usage, however," he said wryly. "I must teach you the familiar tense."

Her eyebrows arched. "Oh? When?"

He brushed his cheek against hers. "Not now," he chuckled.

He took her hand and turned her toward a shuttle. "We have more important and immediate issues to resolve."

CHAPTER NINE

LATER THAT EVENING, after the occupants of the suite shared a meal, there was a startling development. Chacon was not in the room assigned to him at bedtime, nor could he be located nearby in the city. There was only a cryptic message scrawled on a vidpad on the table next to his bed. It consisted of one word. "Dacerius."

Dtimun contacted Patch, who confirmed Chacon's apprehension by parties mostly unknown and his transport to Dacerius.

"I was going to contact you," Patch replied over the vidlink. "I didn't know until an hour ago that it was going down. I've been trying to track his destination. I'm sorry it's taken so long."

"I appreciate your honesty," Dtimun replied, and he smiled. "Before I met you, I did not expect to see nobility in pirates."

"Pirates have families and come from all sorts of backgrounds," Patch told him. "I came from Terravegan nobility. My forebears were titled."

Which explained a lot, Dtimun thought.

"I can at least tell you where they've taken him. I'm downloading a map to your recorder. And be wary. There are high level Rojok military involved, and they have mercs working for them who have sensor webs, they can appear invisible until they attack."

"I am grateful for your help."

"Just don't let it get around, would you?" the pirate asked plaintively. "What will people think if they hear that I've been doing good deeds? It's bad for my reputation."

Dtimun assured him that he would keep the knowledge to himself. Armed with the map, he approached the others, including Princess Lyceria, who was horrified when she heard that Chacon had gone missing.

"But he was here earlier… I spoke with him just after our meal!" Princess Lyceria exclaimed. Her eyes were deep blue with sadness and concern. She and Chacon had spoken privately; she wasn't sharing that knowledge. He'd said nothing about leaving, however.

Dtimun turned to Sfilla. "Do you know anything about this?"

She nodded solemnly. "There was a flash just before he went missing. I was not in time to intercept it, but I am certain that it came from a person whom the Rojok commander-in-chief trusts, because it was on a private frequency."

"Lieumek?" Madeline asked Dtimun.

His lips compressed. "Possibly. However, he is one of Chacon's oldest and most trusted friends. I cannot see him in the role of traitor."

"Keep your friends close, but your enemies closer," Madeline quoted a maxim from old Earth.

Three Cehn-Tahr glanced at her. Two of them read her mind and laughed aloud.

"Well, what do we do now?" Madeline asked.

"Where did the signal originate?" Dtimun asked Sfilla.

"On Dacerius," Sfilla told him.

Dtimun was quiet and thoughtful. "Which is where our contact confirmed that Chacon had been taken. If Chacon were to be enslaved, that would be the best place to conceal it. The Dacerians, for all their pride and high culture, do not see slavery as an issue."

Madeline was reminded of the Dacerian slave women who frequently appeared on the intergalactic market. She thought of it with distaste.

"What do we do now?" she asked.

Dtimun moved away, pacing. "I have a map of the area where he is being held. It will take a little time to make arrangements."

"I'll start on them immediately," Sfilla promised.

"I will take Sfilla and go to Dacerius, first thing in the morning, to free him…"

"Not without me, you won't," Madeline said at once.

Dtimun whirled. "You will not go," he said firmly. "The child makes you too vulnerable."

"Yes, well, the child and I are the only protection you're likely to have," she returned stubbornly. "A lone Cehn-Tahr male in that thieves' den would be immediately suspect."

"She is right," Lyceria commented.

"Bataashe!" Dtimun shot at her, with no regard whatsoever for her position.

Madeline was surprised that the princess allowed him to speak to her in such a way. She glared at her commander. "You shouldn't speak to her that way. She's a princess," she reminded him.

Lyceria's eyes, unaccountably, flashed green at the human female's defense, but she didn't say a word.

"I do not need protection," Dtimun continued, unabashed.

Madeline gave him a droll look. "It will be easier for us to retrieve you if you don't end up in a Rojok prison camp."

"I will remind you that I have lived successfully for two hundred and fifty years without your intervention," he reminded her curtly.

"Lucky you!" she shot back. "I'm going with you."

He moved toward her. "The child will inhibit your ability to protect yourself. The distraction of protecting you could cost us both our lives, to say nothing of the child you carry."

She stared at him. "The child is temporary," she reminded him, "and I won't remember any of this in about two weeks' time."

His eyes made an odd combination of colors and there was a stifled sound from Lyceria.

Madeline glanced at her and frowned. "Are the two of you keeping something from me?" she wondered aloud.

"You and Lyceria will return to Memcache," Dtimun began.

"Like bloody hell I will," Madeline said, standing taller. "You are not going to Dacerius without me!"

"Madam…!"

"Try it," she replied hotly. "You can lock me up, but I'll just escape and find an alternate route to Dacerius and go, anyway."

Lyceria's eyes were mirthful. Sfilla was struggling not to laugh. The commander looked like every male since the beginning of time who was trying to reason with an unreasonable female.

"The child should not go into such danger," he groaned.

She moved right up to him. "Yes, well, unfortunately he and I are a matched set. It isn't possible to leave him behind." Her eyes searched his. "I'm not letting you commit suicide, sir. I put too much work into saving you at *Ahkmau*."

He actually groaned aloud. "Madeline, I do not need the constant reminder…"

"Apparently you do!" She glared at him stubbornly. "I'm going with you!"

Sfilla placed a gentle hand on his arm. "She is correct. If you and I go alone, suspicion will be immediate and possibly fatal."

"Yes, and her son would agree with her," Lyceria said.

"Her son?" Madeline asked, curious.

"My son is captain of the *kehmatemer*," Sfilla replied, smiling at Madeline's surprise.

"Captain Rhemun?" Madeline said aloud. She laughed. "Well, now I know who he gets it from."

Sfilla frowned. "Gets it from?"

"His audacity," Madeline said, and grinned.

"I see," Sfilla responded with a laugh.

Dtimun did not like Madeline's reference to the captain, of whom he had still some small jealousy. He growled softly.

She arched her eyebrows. "Sir!" she admonished.

He averted his gaze.

"We're still dancing around the issue," Madeline said. "You have to let me go with you."

He didn't like the idea, but he was persuaded that she was correct. He sighed. "Perhaps I do." His eyes twinkled. "Hazheen Kamon will permit us to stay in his camp while we search for Chacon. He will provide any additional security that we require."

Madeline was recalling that it had been in that camp where Dtimun had become involved with the Dacerian woman with whom he bonded so long ago. Jealousy rose in her throat like bile. She didn't dare oppose him, because he knew Dacerius far better than she did. But he would be enmeshed in the past there, in his memories of the beautiful Dacerian woman whom he had loved. Madeline would fade into the background, perhaps even be resented by him. She turned away, sick at heart.

He read those thoughts in her mind with surprise. He hadn't thought of the Dacerian woman in some time; certainly not since Madeline had become pregnant and he had realized that his old paramour never was. He started to speak to her, when a flash came over his comm unit.

It was Patch. "I have more information," he said, and related it.

MADELINE WAS RESTLESS. She shouldn't have been. Everything was in place. They knew where Chacon was. Very early in the morning, when their covert transport was ready, they'd go to Dacerius and with the help of Sfilla's operatives, rescue him and secure the future.

And it sounded good. But she, like most military vets, knew that any battle plan, regardless of its genius, was written in water. So many factors could influence its success.

She laid a hand on her swollen belly, on her child. It

was incredible how much she'd changed in the past few weeks. All her life, she'd been a neuter, neither male nor female, only with the appearance of a female, conditioned to see males as comrades, not potential mates. Now everything had changed.

The child inside her had softened her, made her vulnerable, but had also made her stronger. She felt whole now, as she never had before. She dreamed of a future that would give her the opportunity to see her child born, to see him grow into a man, to be part of the family he might one day have.

She smiled sadly. Dreams. Only dreams. Even if she could bear the child without dying, he would be a hybrid. As any biologist knew, hybrids were almost always sterile. It would be impossible…

"Are you pacing again?"

Dtimun's deep voice came from his suite of rooms. Laughing softly, she went to the open doorway and peeked in. He was lying on his side, dressed in that odd Khan-Bo flared pant he wore to sleep in. His broad chest was bare, his hair mussed. He was watching her with faint amusement. He was so handsome that her heart skipped, just looking at him.

"Yes, I'm pacing. Sorry if I woke you," she apologized.

"I was not asleep. Come and sit down. No, not there. Here, beside me."

She moved to the bed and sank down beside him, cross-legged on the bed. His arm went easily around her, his big hand soothing as it moved on her back. Amazing, she thought, how comfortable they were with each other these days.

"I was tormenting myself with the future," she confessed with a rueful smile. "I know better. I just can't help it."

He smiled. He rolled over onto his back and looked up at her lovely face in its frame of tousled long, red-gold hair. "Human nature, I believe your species calls it."

"Something like that."

"You must not brood so much," he said gently. "There are forces at work which we cannot control. The future is not written in stone."

"Yes, that's what worries me…"

"Not Chacon's," he corrected. "Our future."

Her heart jumped. "You said that there was no way," she began.

He smiled. "Yes, I did. I said many things."

She lifted an eyebrow. "You're never wrong. I read it in a military brief somewhere."

He chuckled deeply. "I had a view of the future that may have been unnecessarily pessimistic," he replied. "I have lived through many tragedies in my long life. They have combined to make me cautious."

She studied his handsome face quietly. "The Dacerian woman," she guessed.

He smiled. "No. She was an illusion. There was no pregnancy. She would not have risked her life to save mine. She was an operative sent to assassinate me."

She caught her breath audibly. "An assassin? But how do you know?"

"My father told me. It has taken over six decades for me to listen to him." He sighed and stared at the ceiling. "I hope that I will be more flexible with my own children."

His children. Those he would have one day with a

Cehn-Tahr woman, the children who could inherit his titles and his lands. She put her hand protectively over her stomach.

He glanced at her. "You make assumptions," he accused. "You must try not to anticipate tomorrow."

She shrugged. "Force of habit."

He reached out and touched her cheek lightly. His eyes were that soft shade of gold shown only to family. "There is always hope," he said. "And that is all I can say. When this is over, we will speak again of the future."

"It will be too late," she told him.

He smiled. "It is never too late. And you must rest. Tomorrow will be hectic."

She started to get up, but he tugged her down beside him and folded her close, pulling the sheet up over her protectively.

"You will not look at me, and you will not touch me," he told her firmly as he turned her so that her back was against his chest.

"Why?"

His teeth nipped lightly at the juncture of her neck and throat. "Cats are frightening in the dark."

She laughed like a girl. "You're not frightening. Not anymore."

"We will not tempt fate. Go to sleep."

She drew in a long, happy breath and closed her eyes. "I won't faint if I see you," she pointed out. "I'm a combat veteran."

"We will also not argue."

"Darn," she muttered. "Takes all the fun out of life."

He chuckled. "Our battles have been memorable."

"Yes." Her hand smoothed over his where it rested over the mound of their child. "And long."

His face nuzzled against her hair. It smelled of a light, floral shampoo. He smiled. "You lost most of those battles," he taunted.

"Only because you outranked me," she pointed out.

He shrugged. "Go to sleep. I have no intention of losing another argument." There was a smile in his deep voice.

She laughed. She closed her eyes with a sigh and thought that she'd never been so happy. She refused to think ahead, to a time when she would not be pregnant, when she would forget all these wonderful times with him, even in the face of great danger. Live for the moment, she told herself.

"Yes," his deep voice came into her thoughts. "Only for the moment."

She didn't expect to sleep. But she did, and soundly for once.

MADELINE AWOKE IN the middle of the night. She didn't know why she'd suddenly opened her eyes. Perhaps it was a noise from outside. Whatever it was, she was wide-awake. She realized that she wasn't in her own bed. Then she noticed the long, muscular arm draped over her waist. Odd, the way the hand looked. Not the fingers so much as the size of the hand, and the arm. Frowning, she turned over before she remembered that she'd been told not to.

Her eyes widened. This wasn't the commander as he usually looked. Not at all. This being was huge. Tall, powerful, massive. His face was very like the one he showed to other people, except that his nose was a little broader. But his hair was rayed around his head like a long lion's mane, black and thick, and his ears sat just a little higher up on the sides of his head than a human's. He had a mustache and very short beard, which were like a depiction of ancient Asian humans she'd seen in history vids, the mustache thin and wispy, the beard bare and continuing up to just below his ears. He looked very impressive. Magnificent. She studied him with warm, soft eyes. He was sound asleep, completely oblivious to her scrutiny. This explained the dark room after the bonding ceremony, and his stern warning not to look or touch. He must employ an indentity screen, a sensor net, of some sort—perhaps that was why the microcyborgs were used—so that he wasn't revealed to outworlders. This was the secret he kept from her.

Why? she wondered. Did he think she might become afraid of him, if she saw him like this? Odd, but then, his mind worked differently from hers. It would never matter how he looked. He was Dtimun.

One of her hands slid over his shoulder and encountered the wide band of fur that she had first felt at their bonding, lying against his spine. It seemed to run from the base of his neck and down, probably to the sacrum, perhaps lower. This was one of the differences he was reluctant to share with her, a feline characteristic that, like the brutal mating ritual, shamed the Cehn-Tahr. She was sad that he was so reluctant to tell her. Surely he knew that it would make no difference to her feelings. Or did he know? For a few seconds, she toyed with the idea of waking him and telling him that she knew the truth. But that was unwise. Their relationship was fragile at the moment and it was not the time for confrontations.

She withdrew her hand from his spine. Smiling, she buried her fingers in his mane and slid her face under his chin. Feeling safe, and warm, and secure as his arms closed around her obliviously, she went right back to sleep.

DTIMUN FELT AN unusual sensation. He opened his eyes and started when he saw Madeline. Disobediently she had turned into his arms. She was pressed close against him, her hands tangled in his mane, her face in his throat. She was sleeping.

The fire-haired physician of their early days on the *Morcai* together would never have curled against him like this, or been in any way submissive to him. But the child had changed her. She was another person now; just as strong, just as stubborn, but not the same.

He felt her soft breath on his throat. She slept as if nothing could harm her, as if she felt safe so close to him. A wave of tenderness washed over him. She depended on him, not as her commander, but as her mate. She looked to him for comfort, for security. It made him feel odd. He couldn't remember such a feeling in his life before Madeline, certainly not with the Dacerian woman with whom he had been infatuated so long ago.

He should turn her back around, in case she woke. But the delight of her position was too seductive. He would surely wake before she did, before she saw him and turned away from him, ran from him, as humans had before when they saw his true appearance. He did not want to frighten her, especially now. But the temptation to hold her this way was too great. He gave in to it. He closed his eyes and went back to sleep.

DTIMUN AND MADELINE took a shuttle from Benaski Port to Dacerius. When they landed at the spaceport, another shuttle took them down to the planet's surface. Sfilla had taken alternate transportation, by routes she refused to disclose, presumably to connect with her network of spies. But before she left, she and Madeline had shared a brief talk and Sfilla had taught her another useful mind trick, to keep Dtimun from knowing that she had seen his true face.

Madeline, who had rarely set foot on the desert planet, was fascinated by the colorful and noisy atmosphere. Nomads in sweeping robes wandered the narrow streets between flat adobe buildings, with a constant chatter. A boy passed by them, carrying a large wooden tray atop his head which held loaves of risen bread. Madeline stared after him, curious.

"There is a public oven in the village," Dtimun explained with a smile. "Each family sends its bread to be baked there."

"How do they know which is which?" she asked.

"By a mark that is unique to each family."

"Oh." Her attention was drawn to a Dacerian standing by the gate, holding a huge silvery Yomuth by its reins. The animal resembled vids of extinct hamsters from Earth, except that it was the size of an elephant. Madeline had ridden one once. They were surprisingly fast, and very affectionate to their owners.

"He's beautiful," she told Dtimun.

"He is the pride of Hazheen Kamon's stable," he said surprisingly, and with a flash of green eyes. "It is a mark of honor that he sent it to fetch us."

He spoke to the handler, who grinned and handed him the reins.

Madeline was faintly apprehensive.

"Comcaashe," Dtimun said softly. He coaxed the animal to its knees, lifted her into the padded saddle and leaped up behind her. "We are in your debt," he told the handler, who grinned and saluted him.

And they were off. Madeline felt Dtimun's body, solid and warm at her back, as the animal galloped down the long dusty road.

"You have a question," he remarked.

She laughed. "Well, yes. It's that term, *comcaashe.* You use *camaashe,* as a rule…"

"Comcaashe is the familiar tense," he said at her ear. "It is used only among those for whom we have affection."

She felt the distinction with pleasure. "What does it mean?"

"Difficult to translate. Our language has layers of meaning. However, the closest approximation is 'be still, you are safe.'"

She smiled. "I like it."

He chuckled.

It was difficult to talk with yellow dust flying up from the animal's huge pads, so she leaned forward and closed her eyes, enjoying the rush of wind and the speed. In no time, it seemed, they were at the Dacerian village of which Hazheen Kamon was head man.

Hazheen greeted them with affection. He shook his head when he saw Madeline's distended abdomen.

"I would never have believed that was possible," he told her.

She laughed. "Neither would I, and I'm a doctor."

"Have you had word from Sfilla?" he asked the desert chieftain in a low tone.

Hazheen sobered. "Yes. She and her operatives are in the mountains as we speak. She had intel about the location of a small Rojok base." He shook his head with a heavy sigh. "It is not a thing of which I am proud, that some of my people deal in such kidnappings. Chacon has been a friend to us for many years. I would not want to be responsible for his death."

"Nor would I," Dtimun agreed.

Hazheen looked at Madeline worriedly. "It is dangerous for you to be here, in such a condition," he began.

"A point which I made repeatedly before we left Benaski Port," Dtimun replied tersely. "It was not possible to deter her without a length of rope and a secure room."

Madeline grinned.

Hazheen laughed. "A woman of spirit. It would take such a woman to tolerate your mate," he assured her. "He is used to command."

"I do obey him from time to time," she said, defensively.

"When it suits you," her mate commented.

"Now, now, sir, life would be boring if I obeyed every order you gave me. Tedious, even. And I always obey the really important orders," she added cheekily. She grinned.

"The child is a great danger for both of you," the chieftain said gently. "If his existence were known…"

"It will not be," Dtimun interrupted. "I must speak with your tracker."

"At once," Hazheen agreed. "Come. My amenities are few, but you are most welcome to share what we have."

Madeline was touched. "Thank you."

He smiled at her. "Dtimun has been like a second

son to me," he told her gently, and he smiled. "I am delighted that you have bonded with him."

"It's not permanent, sir," she began.

He pursed his lips and asked, "Is it not?" He led the way into his tent.

THE TRACKER WAS taciturn and helpful. Yes, he knew where the Rojok camp was located. And yes, there was a high level prisoner there. He had been betrayed by one of his own men, who had a Dacerian paramour in another camp.

"We need a battle plan," Madeline remarked.

Dtimun smiled at her. "And I have one. But first we must wait to hear from Sfilla."

"A formidable assassin," Hazheen said soberly. "She is well-known in the three galaxies for her efficiency."

"She has saved my life more than once," Dtimun agreed.

THEY WAITED UNTIL NIGHTFALL. There was no word from Sfilla. Dtimun paced the small tent he and Madeline had been given.

She studied him quietly from a prone position. The child's growth spurts were coming closer together. She had real fears about going into premature labor, despite the drugs Caneese and Hahnson had provided. She tried to keep that knowledge from Dtimun. He had enough on his mind already.

She started to speak when there was a soft chime from his communicator ring. He activated it, and Sfilla appeared, full sized, in the tent.

"I have found him," she announced. "We are in the process of liberating him."

"Admirable speed," he commented. "Hazheen's tracker will lead us to you."

"Take care, there may be small pockets of Rojoks which we have not found," she cautioned, and her image vanished.

Dtimun turned to Madeline. "You should remain here."

She got to her feet and stared at him stubbornly.

He shook his head. "Very well. But this is not my wish."

She smiled and moved closer. "I would not be interesting if I were complacent."

He laughed and impulsively hugged her close. "I must agree."

His easy affection made her feel warm inside. She didn't dare think ahead, to a time when she'd never see him, or even remember these precious few weeks they'd had together.

"Do we walk or ride?" she asked.

"Walk. A Yomuth would be far too noisy, especially at night, when sound magnifies. In case there are Rojok patrols, we must use caution." He paused at the door of the tent, went back inside and returned with two no-vapens. He handed one to her.

She was surprised. "You're arming me?" she asked, stunned. "After all those threats you made?"

"You are not on active duty at the moment and your life might depend on having a weapon," he returned. He glared at her. "This is not, however, an avowal of your own position on medics being armed in the field."

She saluted him.

He shook his head and went out the door.

THE TRACKER LED them through the starry darkness up old desert trails, down thorny paths, on a journey that seemed to take forever.

"It is only just ahead," he whispered finally, and moved into a clearing.

He dropped like a rock. Five Rojok soldiers appeared out of seemingly thin air, surrounding Madeline and Dtimun. One of them had a tiny pulse-syringe which he jabbed against Dtimun's neck. The effect was instant. Madeline watched with horror as her commanding officer became first dazed and then docile.

"And now," the Rojok squad leader said with a cold smile, "you are our prisoners. In one coup, we have captured two of the Tri-Galaxy Fleet's finest officers. And in less than two hours, you will both be dead."

CHAPTER TEN

MADELINE FELT THE bonds tighten every time she tried to free her hands. It was no use. She rebelled at the thought that she would die with her child still breathing in her belly, that Dtimun would die with her. This was not how she had envisioned her death. She only wanted a weapon. Damn the Rojoks!

She looked beside her at Dtimun and grimaced. He was drugged. He could have freed them with a thought if he hadn't been. Which led her to worry about who had known of his mental abilities and told these assassins to drug him. Chacon knew that Dtimun was a telepath, but he would never have betrayed that knowledge. However, there had been a woman in the village who had been quite curious about the Cehn-Tahr male in her camp. There were Dacerian telepaths. Perhaps that woman had been one.

But her suspicions wouldn't matter anymore, not if they died here. She thought of the child she would never see, of a future she had hoped so hungrily for, even when she knew it would be denied. Her green eyes swept lovingly over her mate, her commander, her friend. She had sacrificed so much to keep him alive. It wasn't fair that it should end like this!

"Sir," she whispered. "Sir!"

He opened his eyes and blinked. He stared at her,

DIANA PALMER

his sluggish mind trying to wrap itself around the grim reality of their situation. It hit him immediately. The Rojoks were going to kill them. He could hear them discussing it nearby. He could not manage enough psychic ability to overcome them, in this condition. Madeline would die, along with the child in her womb. The sickness he felt in his very soul was so shocking that his face paled. The thought of losing her now was unbearable.

"Sir, you can escape," Madeline told him urgently in the few seconds they were left alone while the Rojoks debated the best means of dealing with their bodies following the executions.

He glared down at her. "No."

"Listen to me," she said, almost in anguish, "you're one of the finest strategists we have. I'm just a grunt, a common soldier, easily replaced, but you have the experience and the means to help end the war, defeat the Rojok alliance. I know you can get out of here. Even drugged, you're strong enough to break those bonds. Not one of the Rojoks could outrun you!"

He didn't speak.

"It would free you, of the bonding ties," she continued feverishly. "Afterward, you can bond with a Cchn-Tahr woman, an aristocrat, and have children to inherit your lands and titles…!"

"I will not leave you."

"Please!" She saw the Rojoks making preparations. "There's no time. Please. Please go!" Her voice broke on the last word. Her courage had held up, until now, until death was a taste in her mouth. Tears dimmed him in her vision. "Don't risk everything, don't let a scraggly band of Rojoks kill you because of your sense of honor! I'm expendable! Any soldier is!"

His eyes were a soft, quiet golden hue. They searched hers. His face seemed to clench as he looked down at her. "Madeline," he said quietly, "I will not live without you."

The impact of those words was visible. Tears slid, hot and salty, down her flushed cheeks. Her lower lip trembled.

He drew in a rough breath and struggled to regain the control of his emotions that the drug had cost him. "You are Holconcom. You must stop weeping," he muttered. "It is undignified, especially in front of Rojoks."

A helpless laugh escaped her tight throat. "Yes, sir. Sorry." She swallowed. Her throat was dry. "I wish we could have saved Chacon. I suppose it was hopeless from the beginning," she said.

His eyes went that odd opaque blue that indicated mental linking. "Something has gone right, at least," he thought to her. "Sfilla and her people have liberated Chacon. He is safe."

"Thank goodness," she said, straightening. "The timeline will be secure, then."

He studied her. "I wonder." He frowned. "Do you not think it odd that Komak did not mention our deaths? Surely he saw this."

She met his look with curiosity. "You're right, he didn't say anything." She glanced at the approaching Rojoks. She sighed. "Well, I suppose he didn't want to upset us by mentioning that we were going to die saving Chacon." She searched his eyes hungrily. "It has been the greatest honor, and pleasure, of my life, to have served with you, sir," she said formally, straightening.

"And mine, to have served with you."

She bit her lower lip. "I'd give half my retirement for a *gresham*."

He was suddenly still. His indrawn breath was audible.

She looked up at him, frowning. "What is it?"

His eyes met hers. They were…green!

"Okay, now, what's going on?" she asked.

There was a whisper of wind, a skirl of red sand. The Rojoks, moving toward them with intent, suddenly stopped, dead.

All around, flashes of white solidified into Nagaashe. Dozens of Nagaashe. The ones Madeline remembered from Akaashe would have been dwarfed by these. They were as tall as a two-story building, coiled, and they were all spreading their hoods and hissing at the Rojoks.

"Your people have a saying, from centuries past," Dtimun commented blandly. "Something about a group called the cavalry coming over the hill…?"

She burst out laughing. "Yes!" Although she was certain that it didn't refer to white snakes the height of a building.

The Rojoks were running and screaming. In minutes, the heavily armed camp was deserted. A few of the serpents had pursued the fleeing enemy. The tallest, and oldest, of the others undulated over to where Dtimun and Madeline were secured to their posts by chains. He closed his blue eyes for a second and the chains fell away as if by magic. Had Dtimun not been drugged, Madeline mused, he could have done the same.

"We are greatly in your debt," Dtimun thought to him. "But I do not understand how or why you are here."

The white serpent laughed. "Old man in Dectat contacted us. Treaty we signed with him has clause for mutual aid."

"Thank you," Madeline said aloud. Her hand went protectively to her belly. "I thought we were dead."

The serpent lowered his head and looked into her green eyes. "Child will be greatest link between your world and ours and the Cehn-Tahr," he said surprisingly. "Because of child, new worlds will be open to exploration for both your peoples."

Madeline was very still. "You don't understand," she began quietly, and thought about the regression of the child and her own upcoming mind wipe.

"You will see," the serpent murmured.

"We're very grateful to you for saving us," she said again. Perhaps her thoughts hadn't been understandable to him.

The serpent nodded. "You saved our great-grandchild on Memcache," he thought to her. "Family is everything to us. You are now family. You are part of our tribe. You belong to us. So does your mate, and so will your child."

She was sure that no human had ever been so honored. It was a special mark of distinction, since she already owed her life to this tribe of serpents following the crash on their home planet when she had been so near death. Not to mention for getting her damaged ship to the ground in one piece. She smiled, delighted. "It is a great honor. Thank you!"

"You must bring your child to Akaashe to see us one day."

Before she could tell him again that there wouldn't be a child, he undulated back to Dtimun. The serpent had said that the Dectat had contacted the Nagaashe.

They knew Dtimun had been kidnapped, but perhaps they didn't know about the child. She had to hope so. It would be unbearable to have been spared from death at the hands of the Rojoks only to have Dtimun killed by his own people for his relationship with Madeline—even though it had saved Princess Lyceria from likely the same fate as Chacon.

THERE WAS A strange remoteness on the part of Dtimun once they were reunited with Sfilla and on their way back to Hazheen Kamon's camp. Perhaps his lack of control had unsettled him. She supposed his comment had been a last act of kindness, something to make death easier for her. She didn't really believe that he didn't want to live without her.

Chacon was waiting when they arrived. He laughed wholeheartedly at the sight of them, dusty and be-grimed, their garments streaked and torn.

"You look like refugees," he commented.

Madeline gave him a similar appraisal, noting the bruises and abrasions on his dusky skin, the dusty long blond hair and torn shirt and trousers. "Begging your pardon, sir, but you don't look a whole lot better than we do."

"I must agree." He locked forearms with Dtimun and gave them both an affectionate smile. "You have risked much to save me. I am forever in your debt."

"I still have to save you one more time for us to be even, sir," Madeline replied with a grin.

"We can consider that you are, Ruszel. You are for-getting that you saved me when you removed the sniper on Benaski Port."

"We know that Lieumek betrayed you," Dtimun said, solemn now. "I am sorry."

Chacon's eyes twinkled. "Actually he was working on orders from me."

"What?" Madeline burst out.

"We knew there was a traitor, but not whom. Lieumek has a female paramour who is Dacerian, who also has ties to Chan Ho's assassins. He permitted her to think that she could manipulate him. The plot was revealed slowly, but entirely. I allowed myself to be brought here, where we already had operatives in place. Unfortunately it was she who gleaned information about your mental abilities and told the other Rojoks who apprehended you. She has been…dealt with, however," he added grimly.

Madeline knew that Chacon was aware of the power of Dtimun's mind—it had saved Lyceria at Ahkmau.

He glanced at Dtimun. "I have never revealed what I know. The Dacerian woman, however, was a telepath and I fear she might have told others. I am sorry for this."

"It is not your fault. Neither is it a problem any longer. Many changes are coming in the future. Good ones."

Changes. Madeline wondered what they were, and why the revelation of his psychic abilities wasn't a concern to him.

Chacon motioned to Sfilla, who came forward grinning with her arm in a sling. He smiled, too. "Your finest assassin here was instrumental in rooting out the ringleaders and, shall we say, removing the threat." He shook his head. "I am gratified that you never sent her to eliminate me," he told Dtimun, tongue in cheek.

"If you think she's formidable, you should meet her son," Madeline interjected.

Dtimun glared at her.

"The captain of the *kehmatemer* is known to us," Chacon chuckled. "We are hopeful that he will never replace Dtimun as leader of the Holconcom."

"That's hardly likely," Madeline replied. She thought of the future then, of her eminent return to the Amazon Division and the end of this happy episode in her life— which she would never remember. Dtimun would return to lead the Holconcom. It would be over. All over. She hadn't realized that it would happen so soon.

Dtimun and Chacon were staring at each other very solemnly. Madeline didn't notice. She was miserable. She straightened and saluted Chacon. "I'm glad you're safe, sir, but I hope you won't mention my part in your rescue," she added with twinkling eyes. "I'm afraid Admiral Mashita might take the news of it badly. You are the enemy, after all, and court-martials are so messy…"

He laughed out loud "You have my word that I will never tell Admiral Mashita."

"I'll go with Sfilla to pack up, sir," she told Dtimun formally, and saluted him, too. She left before he could say what he was thinking.

Chacon became solemn with her exit. "The child… you are going to permit her to remove it, along with her memory of it?"

Dtimun was very quiet. "There are processes at work that I dare not reveal. Even to you."

Chacon lifted a ridged eyebrow. His eyes twinkled. "Plots within plots. Would Ruszel's old fellow be involved in them?"

Dtimun's eyes made a flash of green. "He sent the

Nagaashe to rescue us," he replied. "He could never admit it, of course, without revealing that he had knowledge of an illegal bonding, an illegal pregnancy, and the salvation of our most dangerous enemy commander-in-chief. The Dectat would probably space him for it."

"Unlikely."

Dtimun shrugged.

"You had better make certain that Sfilla follows Ruszel's every footstep," Chacon advised. "She is formidable, also, and she will have plans for her future that you may not be aware of."

"That is what concerns me." He smiled. "The war will end one day."

"I have hopes of this." He hesitated. "Lyceria…"

Dtimun looked at him knowingly. "I sent her back to Memcache before Madeline and I came here with Sfilla. She is safe." He smiled. "Lyceria is like the rest of her family where her affections are concerned—unchangeable."

Chacon grimaced. "She is very young."

"So is Madeline, but it makes no difference."

Chacon smiled. "There will be a scandal in high circles."

"Madeline and I are likely to create a higher one, and soon. You might want to monitor the nexus in the near future."

"A Cehn-Tahr and human child," he said, shaking his head. "It will confound the three galaxies. Many things will change because of it."

Dtimun nodded. "You have no idea how true that is." His eyes flashed a green smile at Chacon. "Please try to avoid future kidnapping attempts. Madeline is unmanageable even under normal circumstances."

"And far more unmanageable under unusual ones," the other alien agreed. "But she is unique."

Dtimun's eyes made a soft brown shade. "Yes. Unique."

THEY TRAVELED ON a commercial ship to the edge of Dacerian space, but the *Morcai* intercepted the vessel and took Madeline and Dtimun on board.

Madeline's condition, easily visible, had a sudden and shocking impact on both Holt Stern and Edris Mallory, whom Hahnson had not told about Madeline's condition.

"It's all right. I'm only a little bit pregnant," Madeline said at once, tongue in cheek.

Edris looked from her colleague to the towering, unapproachable alien commander with absolute shock.

Which was nothing compared to the look that claimed Captain Rhemun's face when he joined them.

Dtimun's eyes narrowed, darkened and he growled ferociously.

Rhemun flushed, snapped to attention and avoided looking at Madeline at all, while the humans struggled not to laugh.

Madeline glanced at her companion, confounded. She hoped that response would leave with the child. She frowned. What if it didn't? Even if she returned to Admiral Mashita, would the commander be left in this condition, vulnerable to his military authority and the Dectat? Would he still be protective of her, wherever she went, when the child was removed? After all, his memory couldn't be wiped, Hahnson had once said.

He glanced down at her. His eyes narrowed. She looked worn and tired and desolate. He calmed at once.

"It has been an ordeal for her," Dtimun told Hahnson. "She will need rest and access to the herbs that Caneese made into a potion for her. Can you supply it?"

"Of course," he said. He smiled at Madeline. "It becomes you."

Madeline didn't smile back. She was trying to muster enough courage to face the ordeal ahead. She straightened. "Strick, the sooner the procedure is done...!"

She stopped because Dtimun swung her up in his arms, turned and carried her down the corridor, to the amusement of their audience.

"This isn't the way to sickbay," she pointed out weakly.

"We are bonded. We live together."

"Yes, but that's what I'm trying to take care of, if you'll just let me," she protested, struggling.

"Desist," he said without looking down at her. "You will upset the child." He glanced at her as they reached his quarters and his eyes flashed green. "You might sing to him in that odd language."

"It isn't odd, it's ancient French, from old Earth, and how did you know about that?" she asked, stunned.

He activated the door with his mind, walked through and closed it. "The child speaks to me."

She caught her breath. She knew the child's emotions, but she had no idea that Dtimun could communicate with his son on such an intelligent level. "No. It's not possible, not at this stage of his growth."

He put her down gently on the bunk and sat down beside her, smoothing her disheveled hair on the narrow pillow. "I assure you that it is."

Tears stung her eyes. It was going to be more of an ordeal than she realized.

"It is time we spoke truth to each other," he said quietly. "The child is not a secret. He is already known both to the emperor and the Dectat…"

"They'll space you!" she burst out.

"They will not," he said, and smiled. "He is the child of Ruszel, who can do no wrong in the emperor's eyes."

"But the emperor doesn't know me. We've never met," she said.

He bent and touched his forehead to hers. "The birth of the child will be eagerly anticipated, not only by my people, but by your people and the Nagaashe, as well."

"My people will space me the minute they hear of it," she retorted. "Ambassador Taylor will send troops all the way to Memcache to have me brought back…!"

"He would not dare," he assured her.

The door opened. "That is true," another voice inserted.

They both turned. The old fellow, with the *kehmatemer* right on his heels, entered the room. He was eating an apple with great enjoyment. Human fruit had been unknown to him until he encountered it on the *Morcai*. He waved the others away. Rhemun pursed his lips with faint amusement as Dtimun sent him a glare and an angry growl before the door closed, shutting them all out.

"You know about the baby," Madeline said, aghast.

The old fellow grinned. "Of course. So does the Dectat. He is most eagerly anticipated."

"But the law…" Madeline persisted.

"The Species Act was repealed two days ago," he said easily. "In fact, it was repealed by acclamation, a rare instance of accord in my government. We felt, in view of your role in making a treaty with the Nagaashe, that it was the least we could do."

"The inheritance laws," Dtimun interrupted solemnly, "it will not matter to me if they still apply. I can serve the government as a military leader. I would prefer this, rather than give up my mate and my child."

Madeline didn't understand what he meant. How did one give up being an aristocrat?

The old fellow gave her an amused smile. "You do not understand what he is offering to give up for you. Later, it will make an impression. However," he added, turning back to Dtimun, "such a sacrifice is not required. The inheritance laws were also changed."

Dtimun's eyebrows arched. "That is a surprise."

The old fellow chuckled. "Indeed. But a pleasant one, I am certain."

"There is another matter," Dtimun said heavily. "Two of them, in fact."

Madeline gave him a droll look. "He thinks that if I see him the way he really is, I'll cut and run away, screaming, like human females in those old entertainment vids." She frowned. "Did you share those ancient Earth vids with him, by any chance?" she asked the old fellow, teasing, because she already knew that he had.

He burst out laughing. "I did, in the distant past. Fortunately for you, neither of us is likely to give them any credit now, having seen you in combat."

"Thanks." She studied them. "Then what were you talking about?"

"Matters that must remain private, for now, I am afraid," the old fellow replied. He turned to Dtimun. "You must tell her," he said in Cehn-Tahr.

"Not yet," Dtimun replied tersely. "I will show her,

before I permit her to make a decision about remaining on Memcache. But as for the other…"

"She will cope," the old fellow said with twinkling eyes.

Dtimun thought about that, and then relaxed. His own eyes went green as they turned to Madeline. "Yes," he said in that same ancient tongue. "I believe she will. Magnificently."

"That is what Komak told me." The old fellow disposed of the apple core in a disintegrator unit and then pulled something from his pocket and showed it to Dtimun. "This is for the two of you," he said, reverting to Standard so that Madeline could understand him, and his face was solemn. "It will come as a great shock, I think. I will keep it until the appropriate time. Komak instructed me not to give it to you until after the bonding ceremony."

Dtimun frowned. "There has already been a bonding ceremony, before I touched Madeline…"

"A public one," the old fellow interrupted. "And soon," he added firmly.

Dtimun's jaw hardened. "This is too soon. I am not ready."

The old fellow put a hand on his shoulder. "None of us is ever ready, when the time comes. Do you think I was, when my command duties were finished and I was forced to become a politician rather than a soldier? Do you think your mother was, when she left her quiet village and was required to become a public figure?"

Madeline, listening, was puzzled. Dtimun had never spoken to her of his mother, although she had suspicions about his relationship with the old one, here.

Dtimun glanced at Madeline. "It will be a different life than you envision," he said quietly.

She looked at him with eyes that worshipped him. "I'd live in a fishing village with you and sew garments with my own hands, if it was required of me."

Dtimun laughed. So did the old fellow. "So would I, with you," he said gently. He glanced at the old one. "She actually tried to get me to abandon her and leave the Rojok camp when they were preparing to execute us," he said.

The old fellow gave her an amused look. "She would certainly have agreed to abandon you, were the circumstances reversed," he said with some irony.

She glared at him. "He's one of our greatest strategists," she pointed out. "I was expendable."

"Not to me," Dtimun replied, smiling warmly.

"Nor to me, or your mother."

Madeline was really frowning now, all at sea.

"I am his father, as you have probably guessed by now," the old fellow told her gently. "And Caneese is his mother."

Madeline's face became radiant. "Really?"

The old fellow nodded. "The two of us have been sharing secrets that Komak was kind enough to relate."

"Secrets?" Dtimun frowned. "Of what sort?"

The old one nodded toward the disc before he put it back in the pocket of his uniform. "Of a surprising nature. I will say no more about it. But you must wait until after the ceremony to view it."

They both looked apprehensively at each other.

"It is a happy secret," the old fellow said, smiling.

"Oh. Okay," Madeline replied.

"Tragedies have separated us," the older alien told

the younger one. "But I hope that your child will mend many wounds."

Dtimun moved forward hesitantly, and put his own hand on his father's shoulder. "I deeply regret my own actions," he said slowly. "I allowed a misconception to place a drawn sword between us."

The old one smiled gently. "Our battles have been memorable. Some have been amusing." His eyes flashed green as he reverted to the ancient Cehn-Tahr tongue to add, "Your order to the Holconcom to refrain from saluting me has been a source of great hilarity among the *kehmatemer*."

Dtimun shifted, self-conscious. "That was regrettable."

"Lokar offered you a medal for taking the life of your brother," the old fellow said sadly in Standard. "I tried to stop him, but I was too late. The Jebob have an odd mind-set about war, as you know."

"I do know. Now."

"I had hoped that you could reason with your brother, that he would listen to you and turn away from the fanatics," the older alien replied. "He was closer to you than to the rest of us. I did not know, I could not have known, that he would force your hand in such a manner as to leave scars on your heart."

Dtimun's jaw clenched. "Nor did I. I also blamed you for that," he said heavily. He shook his head. "Two brothers, dead, years of cold separation between us, between you and Caneese. So many sorrows."

"Yes. They have been greater for Caneese than for either of us, as well. Her own life has been a series of tragedies, beginning with her family's attitude toward her."

Dtimun glanced at Madeline. "They opposed her

desire for higher education. They had, as many of our people had, great prejudices against females in any role that was nontraditional."

Madeline nodded. "I'm a pioneer, I am," she quipped, and then had to explain what a pioneer was, and where the expression came from.

"The Dectat has made you a brigadier general," the old one told her, and grinned at her shock. "They have also given you full citizenship and you will receive the highest military award we can tender, for your part in the Nagaashe treaty as well as saving the life of Princess Lyceria. For the second time," he added drolly.

"I'm very grateful, for all that. But the first was an accident," she said. "And saving the princess was a pleasure."

Something made both sets of alien eyes flash green.

"You're keeping something from me," she said suspiciously.

"Many things, in fact."

She gave the commander a sly look. "So, do I outrank you now?" she asked with a grin.

He laughed. "No."

"Oh, well," she sighed. She put her hand on the mound of her belly. "I'm so glad that we don't have to regress him," she said softly. "I would have mourned for the rest of my life, even with the mind wipe."

Dtimun touched her cheek and laid his forehead against hers. "As would I."

"I will arrange the ceremony. But you should have a few days to recover from this latest ordeal, first," the old one told them. "Meanwhile, there is gossip that Chacon is gathering forces to overthrow Chan Ho," he added.

"A dangerous play," Dtimun remarked.

"Ah, but he has allies. A million mercenaries have hired on with his troops to join in the fight, all campaign veterans from other armies." He leaned forward. "And the rumor is that some of them are Cehn-Tahr!"

Dtimun and Madeline chuckled. Things were looking up. "I think Komak may have been right about the necessity for saving Chacon," Madeline said. "If he overthrows the tyrant, he'll become the political as well as military leader of the Rojok forces. Perhaps there will be peace."

"There will be," the old one agreed. He beamed at them. "Take great care of each other, and my grandchild. I will see you both again at the bonding ceremony. But I was never here," he added firmly. "You did not see me aboard the *Morcai.* And you have no idea how the Nagaashe learned of your plight and rushed to assist you."

Madeline put her hand over her heart. "Sir, you are a figment of my imagination. I swear."

He laughed. He turned and embraced his son, for the first time in decades, delighted that the embrace was returned.

"Farewell," he told them as he left.

Madeline looked up at Dtimun with such joy that she was almost breathless from it. But a hint of her old audacity remained. She pursed her lips. "I want a battalion of female troops," she told him.

He actually groaned.

CHAPTER ELEVEN

MEMCACHE WAS AS green and beautiful as Madeline remembered it. She was happier than she'd ever been in her life, now that there was a future with the commander. Although, many things were still hidden from her.

"You and your father were saying something you didn't want me to understand," she said when they were sprawled on the grass with Rognan the Meg-Raven and Kanthor, the galot, who were maintaining a grudging peace.

"Yes," he replied. He drew in a long breath. "You have not seen me yet, as I truly appear."

"I have."

He frowned. "I would have seen it in your mind."

She smiled secretively. "Sfilla knows how to block people. I didn't even know she was a telepath until we were on the way to Benaski Port. I didn't tell her why I wanted to know, but she taught me." She grimaced. "I thought I'd be going back to active duty after the mission, and that you'd worry that I might tell somebody about what the Cehn-Tahr truly looked like. I didn't want you to worry." She searched his eyes. "The Cehn-Tahr keep so many secrets."

"We have felt that we must." His eyes narrowed. "When did you see me?"

"The night I was restless, pacing the halls and you called me into your room with you. I woke in the middle of the night. The sensor net is weakened when you sleep, isn't it?"

He nodded, frowning. He was remembering that he woke in the night, too, and found her curled up against him. Now he understood.

He drew in a long breath. "I was afraid that you would find my true appearance distasteful. I would have had to live with the memory of it all my life. And when the child was born, he would have no camouflage, so you would have seen my true face in him. That was one reason I did not oppose, at first, your idea to regress him."

"A very timid reaction from a soldier who has faced death so many times," she said drolly.

He smiled. "Yes. But your opinion has always been important to me. No other has ever carried such weight."

She rolled over onto her side, grimacing because the growth spurts were coming closer together and she was uncomfortable. "I don't find anything about you distasteful. I never could."

He stared at her for a minute, deep in thought. Finally, with visible reluctance, he touched a spot on his wrist.

The being lying beside her was enormous. He was tall and muscular, far bigger than any human male. His fingers were shorter, broader, his hands bigger than they had appeared. He had a long black mane around his handsome face. His nose was a little broader than a human's. But otherwise, he looked just as he always had.

She only smiled. He relaxed and touched her face gently.

"You have no fear of me."

"Of course not. I think you look quite handsome," she replied, her eyes warm with affection. She curled into his body and slid her arms around his neck. "I always did, even when it was against regulations."

He drew her close, embracing her hungrily, his face buried in her throat. "I never thought to have such feelings again for a female. I fought them."

"I noticed."

He rubbed his cheek against her hair. "I still keep secrets. This is not the only one."

"Your father said I'd cope. I will."

He closed his eyes. "Yes. You will."

She drew back and looked up at him curiously. "There's just one other thing."

"What?"

She pulled the fabric away from her collarbone and indicated the way he'd marked her. "Women comment on this. They giggle but they won't say why. What does it mean?"

He traced it lightly with his forefinger. His eyes were that soft, incredible shade of gold that indicated great affection. "It is our symbol for infinity. When a male marks a female with it, the symbol becomes a solemn pledge. It is a promise of fidelity. It indicates that regardless of the time we have together, I will never take another mate."

She was shocked. "But…but your life span is so much longer than that of a human. You could live for a century or more after I die," she protested.

He nodded. His eyes searched hers intently.

"You said you were fond of me," she stammered and her voice broke.

He smiled. "I am." He traced her eyebrows.

She was speechless. What he was saying indicated a feeling much more intense than simple affection.

"Komak's injection may have unknown effects in the future," he added gently. "We do not know how long you will live, but Komak said that you are still alive in his time, far in the future. Your lifespan may equal my own. It does not matter, however," he told her. "I will never mate again. I meant what I said, when the Rojoks came to kill us on Dacerius." His face tautened with emotion. "I will not live without you."

She burst into tears and held him very close.

His arms enfolded her. He buried his face in her throat with a rough growl. "I did not wish this to happen," he confessed. "I did not want to be vulnerable again."

She smiled through her tears. "I can understand that. You loved the Dacerian woman…"

"I did not," he whispered at her ear. "I only thought I did. I was very young." He lifted his head and looked into her wet eyes, and smiled. "I know the difference now." He brushed his tongue against her eyelids, licking away the tears. He stiffened. "This is another of those covert feline behaviors. If you find it offensive…"

She pulled his head back down. "Don't be absurd."

"YOU HAVE TO show the crew how the Cehn-Tahr truly appear," she told him a few minutes later. "You have to," she added firmly. "The bonding ceremony won't allow you to be camouflaged. That's why Caneese said the emperor is barring vid recorders from it. The crew can't attend if they aren't allowed to see you as you are."

His jaw clenched. "They will run for the exits and

beg for court-martials so that they do not have to remain in the Holconcom."

"You underestimate their respect for you," she replied. She smiled. "And their affection. They'd all follow you out the air lock if you asked them to. How you truly appear won't matter. I promise."

He gave her a long look.

"I promise," she reiterated.

He sighed. "Very well. I will call a shipwide meeting tomorrow to announce it."

She smiled her approval.

SHE HAD A gown fit for an empress, of a terribly expensive royal blue fabric with real gems sewn into the gold embroidery. Rubies and diamonds and emeralds glittered like tiny suns when she moved, a little heavily, to study herself in the mirror. With her hair pinned on top of her head, and the creamy skin of her neck and shoulders revealed modestly, she was beautiful.

There was a thin silky panel over the mark of bonding which would be removed, she had been told, at the bonding ceremony. The mark of bonding was displayed by females only in rare public events such as this, to prove relationships.

There were no rehearsals for the event, but as she tried on the gown for the final fitting with Caneese, she was given a brief overview of the ceremony, which would take place later in the week.

She turned to Caneese, who had approved the construction of the gown at every stage. The older female nodded with critical appraise.

"It is quite well made," she said to the weavemaster, who bowed and flushed with gratitude at the praise.

"It's fit for royalty, though," Madeline worried. "These are Imperial colors. I thought only the Clan Ala-mantimichar was permitted to wear them. Although the commander wore them to the Altairian reception," she recalled with some curiosity, "and at our first bonding."

Caneese didn't answer her. "The emperor himself approved them for you," Caneese said with sparkling green eyes. "He is quite impressed by you. So are his 'Praetorians.'"

"But they don't know me," she protested.

"They have certainly heard tales of you from the *kehmatemer*," Caneese said, averting her eyes.

"Oh. I hadn't thought of that," Madeline said. She grinned. "It's quite bad for my ego, all this praise."

"You are not a conceited person," Caneese said with praise.

"Not much to be conceited about," Madeline chuck-led.

"We could disagree about that."

She studied the alien woman with warm affection. "It's nice that you share your true appearance with me," she said. "I've only realized that it is an honor. You never reveal yourselves to outworlders. The commander was afraid that I'd run from him. Fat chance," she drawled. "I'd crawl to him on broken glass on my knees," she added with a sigh.

Caneese found the imagery impressive. "You have changed him, as well as the emperor and our government," she said complacently. "As I said, you carry the future within you."

"We're going to name the baby Komak. I wasn't sure, at first, but I do like the name. We were very fond of Komak."

"As was I," the other woman agreed. She frowned. "You still have concerns. I do not pry," she added quickly. "Your thoughts lie on the edge of your consciousness."

Madeline turned, sad. "I'm still a common soldier, and the commander is not only an aristocrat, but quite famous...."

Caneese laughed. "The emperor himself was a common soldier," she confided, "with no aristocratic ties and rough manners. Yet he achieved greatness."

"I'd forgotten that." She brightened. "Thanks. That makes me feel a little better."

"You still underestimate the affection our people have for you," Caneese said. "But it will become apparent. I must—"

Caneese broke off as she heard a chime and moved away. "The dignitaries begin to arrive," she said, interrupting the conversation. "I must be on hand to greet them, and there are still many preparations that must be made. We will have much time to talk, after the ceremony. You are not nervous?"

"I'm shaking in my combat boots," Madeline sighed. "But I'll try not to embarrass you and the commander's father in front of the emperor."

That brought another green laugh from Caneese's eyes. "There is no possibility of that," she assured her. "The emperor and his consort were notorious for the breaking of protocol at every occasion."

"I've heard about the empress," Madeline laughed. "I think she must be a very special person. Not only for ignoring traditions, but for inspiring the emperor to conquer whole solar systems in order to win her."

Caneese had a secret smile. "She was quite flattered. He was an amazing warrior. He still is, despite his age."

"I saw the old fellow as a young Cehn-Tahr soldier, in my mind, when he saved my life on Akaashe," Madeline recalled. "He was very impressive, too."

"Yes. So is your consort."

Madeline laughed. "Nobody is his equal."

"And that is as it should be."

Madeline allowed the assistants to remove the gown. Under it she was wearing brief robes, but she added heavier ones to them, so that she was discreetly covered. "I'll see you at the ceremony day after tomorrow?" Madeline asked. "You and Dtimun's father are both coming?"

Caneese gave her an amused look. "Yes, indeed."

Madeline sighed. "I'm told there's going to be a great crowd of foreign dignitaries and flash media there. Because the commander leads the Holconcom, of course, and is a high military official. I hope I can find you and Dtimun's father in the crowd."

"I would not worry about it," Caneese said drily. "I imagine it will be possible for us to find each other. Even in a crowd."

"I'll be the one in the gorgeous, princess-type gown, standing next to the most attractive warrior in the room. You can't miss me," Madeline said, tongue in cheek.

Caneese laughed like a girl. "I will remember!" she promised.

DTIMUN WAS APPREHENSIVE about confronting the human half of the Holconcom with his true appearance. Despite Madeline's surprising reaction, he worried that some of the crew might rather face court-martial or execution rather than remain with a shipload of such alien creatures as the Cehn-Tahr actually were under their sensor nets.

"You worry about shadows," Madeline said gently when they arrived at the spaceport where he had ordered the crew to assemble aboard the *Morcai*.

"Perhaps." He walked beside her, tall and commanding in his uniform. She was wearing robes. He glanced down at her and smiled. "At least your condition will not shock them. They already know about it."

"Well, the officers do," she corrected, and sighed. "I suppose it will come as a shock to some of the crew."

He chuckled. "It came as a shock to me. Despite Komak's reassurances, I did not think it would be possible for us to breed."

She smiled. "Neither did I, really, but I think he put something in that injection that assured a pregnancy."

He stopped and turned, frowning. "I wish we had been able to ascertain his Clan," he said. "He used the name Maltiche, but there is no such Clan on Memcache."

"In the future, in his time, there might be such a Clan," she pointed out. "I read that the Cehn-Tahr can create Clans in the Dectat to honor especially brave and heroic soldiers."

"Yes, but that has not been done in decades."

"We don't know what they might do in the future."

"True."

They started walking again. "I know that the old fellow, I mean your father, wants us to call the child Komak, and I agreed, because I think it's a wonderful tribute to our fellow crewmate," she added, frowning. "But I don't understand why he would make such a suggestion."

He stopped again, scowling. "He said that Komak had shared knowledge with him that he was not able to share with me. Perhaps he knows some things that we were not permitted to learn."

"Perhaps. I still wonder about that shadowy human DNA in Komak."

"So do I." He chuckled. "Would it not be amusing if your colleague and Rhemun produced a child one day?"

"You think that's who Komak might be?" she wondered aloud.

"If he has human DNA, it is one possibility."

She was having odd random thoughts herself. Her hand went to the growing mound under her robes. She had the odd impression that the child was laughing. She caught her breath. "No. It couldn't be…!" She looked up at Dtimun. "What if he's our descendant?" she exclaimed. "Perhaps a grandson or great-grandson?"

"That is a possibility," he replied. "Perhaps the old fellow will divulge what he knows at some point. And there is the data vid that Komak left with him, for us to view after the ceremony."

"I'd really like to know the truth. I miss Komak," she said quietly.

He hesitated. "So do I," he confessed tautly.

She laughed abruptly.

He turned to her, his eyes questioning.

"The baby laughed. He thinks it's funny!"

"What, that we miss Komak?" he asked, smiling.

"Apparently."

He studied her with warm affection. "Your condition makes you even more beautiful," he said softly. "It pleases me very much that we do not have to regress the child."

"Me, too."

There was a sudden commotion, and Rhemun and Mallory marched out toward them, side by side, both glaring.

"You cannot give them back to the human military," Rhemun began hotly.

"I won't go," Edris Mallory said curtly. "I don't care if Ambassador Taylor sends a squad of assassins after me…!"

Dtimun held up a hand. He looked from one to the other and cocked an eyebrow at Rhemun. "You do not wish the humans to leave?" he asked, surprised. "You have more reason to hate them than any of the rest of our people."

Rhemun, aware of Mallory's sudden curiosity, stared solemnly at his commanding officer. "It has become a tradition, this mixing of cultures and species aboard the *Morcai*. I would not wish to see it fail because of a renegade human's threats."

"Am I missing something?" Madeline asked. "Was there an announcement that I didn't hear?"

"Ambassador Taylor has contacted the Dectat and made threats," Edris said heavily. "He says that if the Cehn-Tahr don't return our people, he'll have his government, our government," she corrected belatedly, "declare a war vote against the Cehn-Tahr."

"Good luck to him," Madeline said, laughing. "He won't get any support from the Terravegan government on that issue."

"Yes, but he can demand our return," Edris began earnestly.

Dtimun held up a hand. "That is what I came here to discuss." He turned to Rhemun. "Have you assembled the humans as I requested?"

Rhemun nodded. "They are all in the modified galley area."

"Then let us go."

Rhemun and Mallory followed them into the ship, running down the long corridor to the galley.

Madeline laughed, panting as she ran. "It's great exercise, but I feel like a Yomuth."

"I recall offering to trade you for one when the Holconcom were dispatched to assist the Dacerians, soon after the unit was formed," Dtimun chuckled. "What a good thing for me that Hazheen Kamon declined."

"Well, he was fond of the Yomuth," Madeline replied, tongue in cheek.

"I was fond of you. I would never have traded you for anything, even then," he confessed, and laughed when she flushed.

THE GALLEY WAS full of humans, and the murmurs of speculation were especially loud. Dtimun entered first. They all snapped to attention. There were many worried faces.

Dtimun moved in front of the group, leaving Madeline to stand with Rhemun and Mallory. "I have heard of your ambassador's threats," he told the humans.

"Just space us, could you?" Holt Stern said miserably. "I'd rather die here than at the hands of that fanatic."

"Me, too," Strick Hahnson seconded. "Dying isn't so bad. I've done it once already," he added.

There was a skirl of laughter.

Higgins stepped forward. "None of us want to leave, sir. My department feels the same way."

"So does my whole damned department, too, sir," Jennings seconded.

There were murmurs of assent from the rest of the humans.

"The emperor himself has been in contact with me," Dtimun said, surprising Madeline as well as the others. "He proposes a solution. The Dectat is prepared to enact an amendment to our constitution, giving full rights of citizenship to all human members of the Holconcom. As citizens of the Cehn-Tahr Empire, you would be beyond the reach of the human military or its governing body."

There were gasps.

"You would do that for us, sir?" Higgins stammered. "I mean, the emperor would? I thought he hated humans!"

"Your devotion to duty, and to me," Dtimun replied, "have altered opinions in my government, and inclined the Dectat toward great changes in policy. Dr. Ruszel has been responsible for much of that, as well."

Eyes turned toward a very pregnant Madeline Ruszel.

"I saw you like that," Stern blurted out. He grimaced as everybody looked at him. "When she was operating on the CO at Ahkmau," he explained, "I had to help, and Komak was acting as blood donor. Somehow, I don't know how, I saw into Komak's mind, and there was a very pregnant Madeline. But the memory just went away, until now."

Madeline didn't reveal that Komak was a telepath. She just grinned. "There are things about Komak that you can't know, just yet, old dear," she told her former captain. "Sorry."

Stern laughed. "There are a lot of things we don't know, apparently," he added with a chuckle as he nodded toward her swollen belly.

"You can bet on that," Hahnson said with a grin.

"We digress," Dtimun began again. He locked his hands behind him. "There are certain things about our culture that we have not revealed to you. There are precedents for this. Once, a group of humans saw us as we truly are, saw us fight as we used to. They did not react well."

Now the speculation grew louder.

"I have been apprehensive about revealing these things to you." He hesitated. "We have grown fond of our human crewmates. You may not wish to remain Holconcom if you see our true appearance."

"Sir, you can't actually believe that?" Holt Stern spoke for all of them. "I mean, we've served with you for almost three years. I think I speak for all of us when I say we'd follow you into the Netherworld if you asked us to."

There were loud affirmatives from the officers and crew.

Dtimun was visibly touched. "It may come as a very great shock, when you see our true appearance."

"No, sir, a very great shock was when we escaped from *Ahkmau* alive," Higgins said. "It won't matter a bit what you look like."

"Not a damned bit," Jennings seconded. There were other murmurs of assent.

Dtimun smiled. "Very well."

He nodded to the Cehn-Tahr contingent of the Holconcom. All at once, including Dtimun, they touched spots on their wrists. And the Cehn-Tahr reverted to their true appearance.

There were faint gasps, and faint murmurs. Dtimun waited, his teeth clenched. But nobody fainted. There was no rush for the exits.

Holt Stern stepped forward and glowered. "Well, isn't that just great?" he said abruptly. "We already knew you could outrun us and outfight us. But now we have to get used to the idea that you're even better looking than us!"

There was a positive roar of laughter. Dtimun and Madeline joined in.

"However," Dtimun told them firmly, "you will not speak of our true appearance in front of outworlders."

Stern grinned. "Not to worry, sir, we Cehn-Tahr can keep a secret."

Another roar of laughter. Madeline glanced at Dtimun covertly. "Told you so," she whispered to him mentally.

He raised an eyebrow and smiled at her. His eyes were blatantly green.

CHAPTER TWELVE

THE HUGE BUILDING was full of people—rather, human-oids—from all over the three galaxies. It wasn't a cathedral, but it reminded Madeline very much of one. She'd seen static vids of old Earth which depicted such structures. It had a high ceiling, and glowed with a soft blue light. Dtimun had told her once that the form of power they used here, based on nuclear energy, gave it that color.

She was nervous. Combat was easy compared to being on public display. She had wished for another small, private ceremony like their original bonding, but he had said that it wasn't possible. His position in the Cehn-Tahr government made it a public event.

She supposed he meant his position as leader of the Holconcom. But it was still odd that she was allowed to wear the colors of Clan Alamantimichar. Still odder that she was given a tiara to match her gown, one which was filled discreetly with dozens of small, incredibly expensive gems.

Her hand went to the soft mound of her stomach. The child was on display in the cut of the gown. Her pregnancy, Caneese had informed her, was of great pride to her mate's Clan (although she never named the Clan). It was proper that it should be displayed.

She peeked in through the huge entrance doors. So

many people! So many races! There—was she seeing
things? No! There were Nagaashe in the crowd. Two of
them, obviously a mated pair. She felt a thrill of pride.
She was certain that the reclusive serpents rarely attended public events with other races. It was truly a
mark of their respect for her, and Dtimun, that they
came. She grinned as she noticed that some of the humans of the Holconcom, notably Weapons Specialist
First Class Jones, were twitchy in proximity to them.

"You must come down the aisle when the music
begins," Dtimun said in her mind. "We have adopted
this part of an ancient human bonding ceremony, in
your honor. Are you nervous?" he teased. "Surely not!
We have been in many great battles together. This is a
peaceful event."

"I would prefer Rojoks and a Gresham," she teased
back.

"If you look carefully, you will note that one of the
Altairian delegation is wearing a sensor net and looks
suspiciously like a Rojok of our acquaintance."

Her heart stopped. "He wouldn't dare…!"

He laughed. "He would. He told me that nothing
would prevent his attendance, not even possible capture. He is fond of you."

She smiled. "I'm fond of him, too. And don't growl.
It isn't that sort of fond."

He chuckled.

She touched her belly softly. "The baby is very restless."

"He does not like crowds," he mused. "Nor do I.
This is very uncomfortable. Like you, I would prefer a
battle. But we have no choice."

"I'll adapt," she promised.

"Yes, of course you will."

She started to say something else, but trumpets sounded. At the far end of the structure, there was a procession. There was a squad of blue-uniformed Cehn-Tahr with Rhemun at its head. They surrounded a party of three, a tall white-headed Cehn-Tahr in jeweled robes, a female with silver hair in a gown similar to Madeline's and a young woman whom Madeline recognized as Princess Lyceria. That would be the emperor and empress. She watched, spellbound, as they moved to a position on a platform reached by a majestic set of wide stone steps. They took their seats in elegant thrones overlooking the ceremony. The rumors that the emperor and his mate were estranged must be false, she concluded. They seemed quite happy together.

"The emperor and his family must value you very highly, to attend our bonding," she told Dtimun. "I'm so flattered!"

He was laughing. "Yes, they do value me. And also you."

She shrugged. "If they did, it would only be because I'm your mate," she said with a smile in her tone. "I'm just a common grunt."

"An undignified and inappropriate term for a female so beautiful and intelligent," he murmured softly. "Did I not tell you, a long time ago, that you would grace a palace? And so you do."

"Is this a palace?" she asked, surprised.

"Yes," he replied. "It serves as a meeting place for the Dectat, as a holy place of worship, and as a home for the imperial family, all together. We do not separate religion from royalty and politics. The three are carefully interwoven in our culture."

She smiled. "I like your culture very much, especially its emphasis on family."

There was another burst of trumpets.

"You must come down the aisle. I will be waiting with two members of our theocracy at the end of it, along with an Allfaith representative from Trimerius."

"An Allfaith—how in the world did he get here? Is Ambassador Taylor in the shadows with a squad of covert operatives waiting to take me into custody?" she worried mentally.

He laughed at the word pictures in her mind. "Ambassador Taylor is being dealt with. You have nothing to fear from him. Nor does our crew aboard the *Morcai*. His days of power are at an end. Quickly, now, move down the aisle."

She bit her lip from nerves and started out into the long carpeted aisle. She was aware of eyes watching her from every corner, and the smiles of her crewmen. She even recognized little Admiral Mashita in the audience, along with Admiral Lawson and other military leaders. Her father had been invited, but he was leading an assault in a far-flung galaxy and was unable to attend. He did send a hologreeting, however, to congratulate them.

The number of dignitaries in the audience was disconcerting to Madeline, especially when she noticed how the imperial family was also watching her. Not only that, she seemed to have an honor escort of Cehn-Tahr soldiers dressed in the same uniform as the *kehmatemer*. Strange to have a military escort at such a time. Perhaps, she reasoned, it was because of her changed relationship to their culture's highest military leader. *Please,* she murmured silently, *don't let me trip over my feet and fall down on the way!* Dtimun heard the thought and chuckled, assuring her that she would not. She was a bit dubious.

But she walked with elegance and pride, and she didn't trip. At the end of the carpet was Dtimun, wearing robes as rich and elegant as her own, and with a crown on his head, like the tiara on hers. He was also wearing the blue and gold colors. The emperor must really like him, she thought as she stopped beside him.

He was laughing outrageously, but silently. The child kicked, as if he, too, were amused. Madeline peeked up at Dtimun and grinned.

The Cehn-Tahr officiating at the ceremony was elderly and had the kindest eyes Madeline had ever seen. He spoke in the old language, the holy tongue, High Cehn-Tahr, in which Madeline had been carefully tutored by Caneese. She understood the phrases that would require her to speak in the affirmative, but much of it was too difficult to decipher.

She and Dtimun joined hands and repeated a certain phrase. The officiant nodded and Dtimun gently uncovered the opening in her gown so that the mark of bonding was visible. Now that she knew what it meant, she was proud to have it displayed.

The officiant pronounced them bonded, welcomed them, and then the Allfaith representative from Trimerius greeted them and spoke a few words about fidelity and blessings and the miracle of childbearing. He pronounced them bonded, as well.

There was a long, sweet fanfare from the trumpets. The audience stood up and members of the various delegations bowed. There was another fanfare and the imperial family stood up and moved down from its position onto the carpeted floor.

"They're coming toward us!" Madeline exclaimed silently. "What do I do? I've never met an emperor or empress before!"

Dtimun was laughing. "You lower your eyes and nod, you do not bow."

"But, look, everybody else is doing it!" she protested.

"You do not bow," he repeated sternly.

She sighed. "Yes, sir."

He groaned.

"Sorry. I'm working on it," she thought with irrepressible humor.

"If you salute me, there will be a scandal," he promised, but amusedly.

She laughed silently. But there was no time to respond. The royal family had moved to face them and stopped. She looked at elegant jeweled gowns and slippered feet, and one pair of big black boots. Her heart was racing. She was so nervous...!

There was deep, familiar laughter. She looked up, right into the eyes of the old fellow. But he wasn't wearing his familiar blue uniform. He was wearing imperial robes of blue and gold, and a crown. A very expensive crown. Caneese was similiarly attired, also wearing a crown, as was the princess.

Madeline hoped she wasn't going to faint. She realized at once what she'd missed all along. The "old fellow" was the emperor. Caneese was his mate, Lyceria his daughter. Around him was the *kehmatemer*, led by Rhemun. And now she knew what that word meant. This was the emperor's Praetorian Guard.

"A surprise, I gather," the emperor told her, with twinkling eyes. "And now you know whose life you saved at Ondar, do you not?" he concluded.

"Sir, I never realized…!" she began.

He touched her cheek and laid his forehead against hers. "It is a great joy to welcome you to my family," he said gently, a comment that Madeline was too surprised to question. "May your years be long and happy and fruitful."

"Thank you," she replied, still stunned.

Caneese repeated the ritual behavior and then hugged her. "What a joyful addition to our family. You have been the means of reuniting it. All of it," she added with a warm glance at her son, standing beside Madeline.

"We are greatly in your debt," Lyceria added, laughing, and she hugged Madeline, too.

That was when it hit her. She looked up at Dtimun, with all the years of comradeship and arguments in her mind as she saw the puzzle pieces join together. He led the Holconcom. But he was also the heir to the throne of the Cehn-Tahr Empire. And she was carrying his heir in her womb.

"So sorry," she whispered as her head began to spin. "But I think I may…" She couldn't get out the word, *faint*, before she demonstrated it.

When she came to, seconds later, Dtimun had her up in his arms, gown and all, and they were standing on the balcony, along with the rest of the family and Holt Stern and Strick Hahnson.

"It's just another burp," Hahnson said as he read his wrist scanner. "She's fine. The excitement, I dare say, has been a little much for her. Especially," he added with a grin toward the emperor, "the revelation of her new status." He shook his head. "I would never have guessed," he told Dtimun. "And I've known you a lot longer than the rest of the crew. Some secret."

Dtimun nodded gravely. "A source of great worry to my parents and siblings," he mused with a smile. "But I went my own way, as I always have."

"And made us greatly proud," the emperor said warmly. He glanced at Rhemun and growled something.

Rhemun grimaced. "Forgive me, sir, I am so used to wearing it that I forget it is on my head."

He pulled off the helmet. A thick, curly wave of black hair cascaded from his head around his broad shoulders and down his back, almost to his waist.

Lieutenant Commander Mallory, just joining the others, stopped in her tracks and just gaped at him with eyes full of wonder.

"Magnificent, is it not?" Caneese was amused at the little blonde human's expression. "The Rojoks have placed a bounty on his head. His men insist that he wears the helmet in battle so that his hair does not show."

"He could cut it," the emperor suggested amusedly.

"There would be bonfires and protests all over the empire," Lyceria teased. "His hair is the glory of his Clan."

"Something his mother would certainly affirm," Madeline chuckled.

Dtimun glanced at her with narrowed eyes. He growled at Rhemun.

Rhemun saluted him, but his eyes were green. "Permission to be dismissed, sir? The refreshment table has *entots* fruit," he added.

"Dismissed," the emperor pronounced.

"If you eat all the fruit again, as you did once before, I will have your head shaved," Dtimun warned.

Rhemun saluted him smartly, grinned and walked

back into the great room where refreshments were being served on a long table with elegant settings. Edris Mallory was still watching him, spellbound, from a distance.

A LITTLE LATER, Madeline was still trying to get over the shock of her new royal relations by marriage when the old fellow, as she still thought of him, joined her with Dtimun and Caneese and Princess Lyceria.

"And now you know why he speaks to me in such a manner when he is angry, yes?" Lyceria laughed, glancing at Dtimun. "He is my brother."

"I speak to everyone in such a manner when I am angry," he said, unperturbed.

The old fellow laughed. "Neither of us is famous for diplomacy. We only practice it in emergencies."

Caneese moved forward, taking her mate's arm. "I agree." She smiled at Madeline. "And now you are truly my daughter. I greet you with welcome and affection."

So saying, she laid her forehead against Madeline's and touched her cheek. Madeline echoed the ritual. It was then performed both with the old fellow and Lyceria.

As Madeline looked at her mate, she realized the enormity of what Dtimun had been willing to sacrifice for her. He had told his father that he would relinquish the throne of an empire rather than give her up. It was humbling. For the first time, she realized that his feelings for her at least equaled hers for him.

"Stern, you and Hahnson can have access to the guest suite," Tnurat told the two humans with a smile. "The weavemaster will provide you with comfortable clothing. Come back and feast with us, and we will trade great lies about our prowess in battle."

"Love to, sir, but you won't have to lie about yours," Holt Stern chuckled.

"I'll second that," Hahnson added. "We'll try to agree on a few lies about our exploits before we return. Won't be long. And congratulations to you both," he added to Madeline and Dtimun.

"Thanks," she said with a warm smile. She would have hugged them, but her mate's eyes were already a soft brown. She decided to cut her losses. They could discuss these little problems later, when they were alone.

"And it is also time that I gave you this," Tnurat added, pressing a small disc into Dtimun's hand, "as I promised."

"What is it?" Madeline asked, curious.

"It is a message which Komak left for you both. I was instructed very strictly about when to present it, and under what circumstances." He hesitated when he saw their worried expressions. "It is a joyful thing," he added gently. "But you should view it together, and apart from the rest of us. It will be, I think, quite emotional."

They gave him a curious look, but agreed to the suggestion.

Later, in Dtimun's suite, he fed the tiny disc into a vidplayer and sat down beside Madeline on a wide chaise while the hologram of Komak suddenly appeared, lifesize, in front of them.

He smiled at their surprise. "This is interactive," he told them. "In the future, our tech has quite surpassed anything that exists now. The program which contains my image allows us to communicate as if I were actually here, even though I am parsecs away in distance and almost a human century away in terms of time."

Madeline was fascinated. "You can hear what we say?"

"Oh, yes. I had keyed the codes before I left the Holconcom, in preparation for this conversation." He sobered. "I was sincerely hopeful that you would be able to hear it. The future was in flux while Chacon was in danger. It delights me that you assured the timeline."

"It was not easy," Dtimun sighed. He looked at Madeline with open affection and smiled. "I had great hopes. It is pleasing to see them finally realized."

"And now you know not only how your commander truly appears," Komak continued, "but who he really is. This must have come as a surprise."

"It came as a shock," Madeline corrected flatly. She glanced at Dtimun and shook her head. "I would never have made the connection."

"No one has in centuries," Dtimun replied quietly. "The only protection the children of a ruler have are scores of bodyguards or anonymity. I have a bodyguard…"

"…which you only use when you're forced," Madeline murmured drily.

"…but I prefer anonymity," he continued, unabashed. "No vids of us are allowed. My face is not known outside the Holconcom. My father insisted on this when we were very young."

"He was wise to do so," Komak replied. "But your identity is now known, which means an end to your career with the Holconcom. I am sorry for this. I know you in the future," he added enigmatically, "but you rarely speak of the adventures you and Madelineruszel had as members of the unit. You are both overly modest in your referrals to service with the Holconcom."

Dtimun frowned. "Do you have human DNA?" he asked bluntly, voicing a question he and Madeline had often discussed.

"Yes," Komak replied, smiling. "Perhaps if you see my true appearance, without the sensor net, many things will become clearer."

He made an adjustment and morphed into the traditional Cehn-Tahr form. His skin was more like Madeline's than Dtimun's. His eyes were human-shaped, although they retained the color-changing ability. The biggest surprise was his hair. It had red highlights, something Madeline had never seen any Cehn-Tahr display.

"You are curious about my hair," he commented when he saw Madeline's puzzlement. "I get it from my mother," he added softly.

"Do we know her?" Dtimun asked.

Komak laughed until his eyes teared. "Yes, you know her quite well."

Dtimun and Madeline exchanged questioning glances. "Mallory's hair is blond, but she might have redheads in her ancestry. I just feel in my bones that she and Rhemun will have a child one day..." Madeline stopped.

Komak was shaking his head.

"They won't?" she asked.

"You have speculated widely about my parentage. I told you before I left," he added to Dtimun, "that we would see each other again, but that you might not recognize me."

"I recall," Dtimun replied. "It was a nebulous response to my question."

Komak's eyes turned that soft shade of gold that Madeline recalled was only used among family. "Even now," he said gently, "my mother carries me in her womb."

He was staring at Madeline. She got the point almost at once. Her hand went to her swollen stomach. Her face paled. She stared at Komak, transfixed.

Dtimun, also, was dumbstruck.

Komak nodded. "I thought it might shock you, when you knew the truth. I have served with you for almost three years. We have wrecked bars together," he told his mother with a very human laugh, "we have fought side by side, endured hardships, had glorious battles with Chacon's forces." His face became solemn. "It is not given to most children to know their parents as equals, as comrades in arms, as friends. I did not realize what a privilege it would be."

His parents moved a little closer together, unconsciously, as they stared at the image of their child as an adult.

"I told you that I made vids of this time period," Komak added, chuckling. "And they truly will entertain you in the future. One of them is of my dignified, elegant mother in the process of bashing a fellow officer over the head with a weapon in a bar brawl." He roared with laughter. "I could not believe what I learned about her, when we served together. You were quite dignified and stoic," he told Dtimun, "just as you are now. But as commander of a combat unit, you surpassed my wildest expectations. I understand now why many of your command theories are studied in military academies all over the three galaxies. You had an unorthodox, elegant style of command which could morph instantly to suit any situation you might encounter." He swallowed. "I have always had affection for you, because you were my father. But as a commanding officer, you are absolutely without peer. It was a great honor to serve with you. A great honor."

Dtimun cleared his throat. "When you were not overly irritating, you were a fine young officer," he said, trying to unbend just a little. His eyes abruptly flashed green. "Although there is the matter of the bar brawls in which you encouraged your mother."

Madeline grinned. "My boy," she murmured proudly. The smile faded. She placed her hand gently over her belly and tears brightened her green, green eyes. "My son," she whispered to the image projected by the vidplayer.

Komak, too, had suspiciously bright eyes. "It was a time of learning for me, in many respects. I now understand the emperor's reluctance to discuss details of these covert operations." He shook his head. "I can barely believe the true story, myself."

"Your grandfather is unorthodox," Dtimun said affectionately. "I learned many of my command tactics from observing vids of his own combat style. You never knew your uncle, Alkasaar. He turned rebel because of the genetic manipulation, to save his son from it. Later, he allowed himself to be killed, to prevent the family from suffering even more anguish over his actions. Then Marcon died on Terramer."

Madeline recalled at once her first meeting with Dtimun on Terramer, as he saw his brother there, dead. She now understood his reaction. She recalled the memorial service she'd attended with Dtimun on Trimerius, as well.

"With Marcon dead," Dtimun continued, "I was left to inherit the throne. I am still not certain that I want it… Why do you laugh?"

"There are still some things I know, which I cannot disclose," Komak told him gently. "Suffice it to say that you will not have to worry about such things for many years. You will have quite enough to do with diplomacy and being a father to me and my siblings."

"Siblings?" Madeline actually stood up, because Dtimun had never disclosed what his father had admitted to him in confidence.

"Oh, yes," Komak said.

Madeline looked at Dtimun with fascination. He smiled.

"Your actions have assured the timeline," Komak continued. "Thanks to you, there will be generations of peace. The future is assured, not only for you two and my grandparents but also for my mate and I, and our sons."

"Your DNA is hybrid," Madeline said slowly. "Are your sons adopted…?"

"They are not," he told her, "and part of their DNA is also human. Which is why I remained a little longer before your bonding ceremony. I wished to gather information for my mate about her parents."

"Rhemun," Madeline guessed.

"Mallory." Dtimun nodded.

Komak roared with laughter. "You are too perceptive. However, I must let you assume some things because I cannot deal in facts. The future is delicate."

Madeline sat back down beside Dtimun. "Can we do this again?"

"Do what?" Komak asked.

"Talk to you like this with the interface?"

He smiled sadly. "That will not be possible. I cannot risk contaminating my own time by saying something unwisely."

"I see." Her face was sad.

Komak took a long moment to look at his parents as, before, he had only seen them in vids made by the Clan, in the future.

"You are not what I expected," he said softly. "I saw only the authority figures and the history. Now I am able to see the real people, in all their dimensions. It was a rare and beautiful glimpse into a world I have only seen in vids, and few of those due to the coronal mass ejection that crippled our libraries and archives."

"I never expected that you would be our child," Madeline replied, her eyes warm and sad, because this would be the last time for many years that she would speak with her son as an adult. "I thought of Mallory and Rhemun instead, because I had planned to return to active duty when we rescued Chacon."

"One should never make plans and expect them not to change with circumstances," Dtimun counseled.

She wrinkled her nose. "Spoken like a true military commander."

"Yes, but that career, and yours, must be sacrificed so that we can raise our son," Dtimun told her with affection. "We will remain on active duty, however. And when the children are older, the emperor has approved your plan for a division of female troops, which you will lead."

Madeline glowed. "What a nice wedding present that was. Like my citizenship," she added.

"Your rescue made possible the Nagaashe treaty," Komak told her. "The Nagaashe will assist you in research in years ahead. They are the key to time travel. I will say no more," he added, smiling. "But all the tech that my generation enjoys has theirs for its basis."

"It's amazing," Madeline said.

He nodded. He glanced from his father to his mother and struggled with emotion. "I will miss you both very much," he said. "But I rejoice in the future that we will all share."

"I can't wait!" Madeline said breathlessly.

Dtimun glowered at the boy. "I know now that your parents must have been quite lenient with you to produce such rebellion and audacity," he began.

Komak held up his hand. "You are not lenient, and I have never been rebellious. I have simply been interesting," he told his father. "Surely you do not wish me to grow up to be taciturn and unapproachable? My grandfather is the emperor, and he can be surprisingly outrageous."

Dtimun looked at Madeline. "Yes, like your mother."

She raised both eyebrows. "I'm not outrageous. I'm interesting." She grinned.

He chuckled. "So you are."

"I must go now," Komak said. He smiled gently at them. "I told you once, but I will repeat it. It has been the greatest joy and privilege of my life to have served with both of you in the Holconcom, to know you as comrades. It is difficult to leave. But the present is where your focus should be now. I leave you with great affection. And I will see you very soon. Farewell and fair sailing, as the humans say." He hesitated. "I love you both, very much."

And he was gone. Madeline's eyes were bursting with tears that she couldn't prevent. Dtimun was very still for a few moments. He would not let Madeline see his face. When he stood up, and noticed her emotional response to Komak's farewell, he pulled her up into his arms and held her very close to him, rocking her in the silence of the room.

"He was our son," she whispered huskily. "Our child."

He smoothed her hair. "I could not be more proud of him," he replied. "I was proud of him when I had no idea that he was my son. He is quite exceptional."

"Yes," she replied softly. "Quite exceptional." She closed her eyes and pressed closer to Dtimun. "The future looks very promising."

He smiled above her head. "Promising," he agreed. His eyes closed as he rested his cheek against her hair. "Promising."

CHAPTER THIRTEEN

WITH SO MUCH going on, Madeline hadn't thought too much recently about childbirth. Her pregnancy, thanks to Komak's mix of genetic materials, had gone quite smoothly, even with the growth spurts. She and Dtimun grew closer, and the more she learned about his culture, the more content she was to live in it. The most important thing was not material wealth or ownership of things. It was family. That was the core of Cehn-Tahr society. There was no money, as such. Each person or family contributed to a fund which was coordinated by machinery that could not be tampered with. Funds were distributed according to need. Greed was almost unknown. Clans lived in great compounds, and were related to Clans all over the planet and in its many independent colonies. Clan members could not marry within the Clan, regardless of the distance. Females might not go to war, but they controlled most of the planet's finances and service organizations. They had great power. Many served in the Dectat, many more were governors of outlying colonies.

However, Madeline would become the first female brigadier general in Cehn-Tahr history, and she made certain that the emperor understood her plans for it. She wanted a combat division, as capable as the Holconcom, with women in positions of command within it. Tnurat rolled his eyes, but he laughed and agreed and pushed the legislation through the Dectat. As Dtimun often said, Madeline could do no wrong in the eyes of the emperor.

Dtimun walked in as Madeline was trying to study a vid on human childbirth, while Rognan and Kanthor looked on with fascination. The Meg-Raven and the galot had been her constant companions since the formal bonding ceremony. Madeline could not go two steps around the estate without her two companions. The emperor was highly amused. Kanthor rarely associated even with Cehn-Tahr and he hated Rognan, but he was quite protective of Dtimun's unborn cub.

Caneese and Rognan had been enemies for decades, but the prospective child had made friends of them. Now, when Caneese worked in her biolabs, Rognan occasionally found his way there to offer her a bit of fruit or a sample of some elusive fauna which she coveted for her experiments. Being part of a family was the most delightful part of Madeline's new relationship. Even her father visited quite often and they grew closer, too.

Dtimun was always nearby. He had new duties in the capital, overseeing imperial concerns of the Dectat, but as Madeline's time drew near he was more often home than not.

He frowned as he stared over Madeline's shoulder at the wall-wide vidscreen. "This is unspeakably disturbing," he said when footage of a human newborn, before it was cleaned up, flashed on the membrane-thin screen.

She glanced at him and grinned. "Yes, but it's part of the process."

"You are feeling all right?" he asked gently.

She laughed and started to stand. "Of course I..." She gasped and doubled over and passed out.

Dtimun had servants covering the room, some dispatched for Hahnson and Mallory, some sent to the court physicians, some to summon the imperial family. He delegated well despite his fears for his mate.

She came to, held close in his arms. His eyes were royal blue with concern.

"I'm okay," she said in a wispy tone. "It's just childbirth, Cehn-Tahr style. I read up on it in your library..." She clenched her teeth. The pain was formidable. "There's no way this child can be born naturally, you know," she managed to say. "He's too big. It will have to be a caesarian section."

"A good thing I kept Hahnson and Mallory from attending Ambassador Taylor's trial," he mused.

She laughed. "I would like to have gone, too. It's the first time in Terravegan history that such a high public official has been tried for treason. He'll be convicted, too. Lawson said Lokar as president of the Tri-Galaxy Council was making sure that there were no bribes or intimidation by publicizing Taylor's long-standing ties to the Rojok Dynasty and his financial benefits gained from them."

"I would have enjoyed spacing him," Dtimun muttered, recalling his anguish when Madeline had been reassigned by Taylor to a frontline combat unit and very nearly killed. Taylor's intimidation had made her rescue impossible after her ship crashed. Dtimun had broken many laws in his efforts to successfully rescue her from Akaashe. He had actually risked his place in the succession for her. She hadn't understood until she

knew who he was. It had been a revelation, an indication of his feelings for her, which he never really voiced.

"I wouldn't mind watching Taylor walk through an
air lock without a suit. But at least he's through making trouble for the military," she agreed. She clenched
her teeth again. "They need…to hurry!"

He called a servant and made threats. He never raised
his voice, but the servant left the room at a dead run.

Madeline could see him in command of an empire,
with ease. He had the ability to inspire not only confidence and loyalty, but immediate action. Today, she
was grateful. She never told him that she was afraid of
the process. But she was.

"I knew," he mused, and took her hand tightly in
his. "You cannot hide your mind from me now. Even
when you try."

"I'll take…more lessons," she threatened.

He managed a laugh.

Hahnson was breathless as he entered the room, followed quickly by Mallory. "We ran the whole way," he
assured them.

He activated his instruments and read Madeline's
condition. "We need everybody out of this room, now,"
he told Dtimun. "And I want fresh, sanitary linen and
a small tub of water."

Dtimun went out to organize those things.

"Yes," Rognan the Meg-Raven croaked, pausing at
Madeline's side. "Old Earth custom. Boil water and
hit baby."

She burst out laughing, through the pain.

"No!" she exclaimed. "There was no hot water on
ancient Earth unless it was boiled. So they boiled hot

water, mixed it with cold water, to make lukewarm water in which to bathe the baby."

"You hit the child, too?" Kanthor, the huge black galot, asked curiously, his feline features almost making an expression of disdain.

She laughed again. "They held the baby up by his ankles and slapped him on the bottom to make sure he breathed when he was first born. That's an older custom."

"Yes," Rognan said proudly, with his new understanding of childbirth. "Boil water, hit baby."

"Out," Dtimun ordered, pointing toward the hallway.

Rognan ruffled his feathers and glared at him. Kanthor sat on his haunches and growled softly with his ears flattened.

"I think that means they aren't leaving," Madeline commented.

"It is unsanitary for them to be in here," he said curtly.

"Germs are everywhere," she pointed out. "They don't have any more than we do, and there are sterile fields already in place. Let them stay," she coaxed. "They're family."

He sighed angrily. But her expression softened his resolve. He sighed. "Yes. I suppose they are."

IT WAS A long process. Painful and exhausting. Even with modern medicine, her vital signs had to be stable before the procedure began. There had been some difficulties with her blood pressure at the end of the pregnancy, and an annoying edema. Despite protocols, Dtimun refused to leave her. His worry was that of all expectant fathers, something no amount of tech could resolve in his mind. His mate and this child had become his world. He brooded, holding tight to Madeline's hand and restraining his protective instincts as Hahnson, necessarily having to touch her, worked to remove the child through a bloodless, very precise incision. But finally, there was a sharp little cry—Hahnson disappointed Rognan by not hitting the baby on the bottom—and Komak came into the world.

Dtimun sat down beside Madeline, whose incision was already closed and flash-healed so that no mark showed on her belly. She was holding the baby in her arms. When she looked up at Dtimun, her eyes were misty.

The child looked like both of them. He had Dtimun's pale golden skin, although it was a lighter shade. He had Madeline's eyes, or rather, the shape of them. When his eyes opened, they did not change color. But the physicians thought they would, when the child was a little older. Certainly the adult Komak's eyes made the same color changes that other Cehn-Tahrs did. He was perfect in every detail. They uncovered him and counted toes and fingers and touched, with wonder, his soft little face.

Dtimun was obviously moved by such a profound experience as parenthood.

"One can read about it for years, but the experience itself is beyond the scope of any words," he said finally, as he traced his son's cheek and smiled.

Madeline thought she'd never seen such an expression on anyone's face before. It was one she'd carry all her life.

She smiled wearily. "He's perfect," she pronounced.

"Yes." He bent and brushed his mouth over her face, as humans did. "Perfect."

THE CHILD WAS christened Komak Maltiche Marcon Alkaasar Ruszel Alamantimichar—named for his father, his uncle, and his grandfathers. Colonel Clinton Ruszel came to the ceremony in full dress uniform with his entire officers' corps in tow. He handed out some odd brown tubes of vegetation whose purpose was unknown. He had located the tradition on a vid and had a replicator fabricate some to pass around. At least one guest ate his and became deathly ill, after which the tubes were simply carried.

News vids were, of course, prohibited, because the Cehn-Tahr did not allow sensor nets in christening ceremonies. But family was allowed, and so were Lawson and Lokar. Old Mardol, who'd loaned them the weapon on Benaski Port, was given the position of godfather, which was a shock and a delight to him, especially when he finally knew the identity of the odd trio who had borrowed his sniper kit. Hazheen Kamon of Dacerius was given a similar role. There was an oddly dressed person who also became the child's godfather, but he was unrecognizable in the garments he wore. Someone whispered that he looked quite like a certain Rojok military leader. But he whispered it only within the family.

As Dtimun stepped down from command of the Holconcom, to take up his duties as heir apparent, Rhemun became the new Holconcom commander. Lieutenant Edris Mallory took Madeline's place as Cularian medical specialist. There were rumors that the two of them were already setting new records for time spent arguing, surpassing even Dtimun and Madeline.

But these things were of little interest to the new parents, sitting on the balcony some time later with their firstborn in Madeline's arms as the two moons of Memcache rose beautiful and haunting in the night sky.

Madeline kissed her son on the brow. "How many parents ever get to know their grown child before he's even born?" she mused, and laughed as she looked at Komak. "Just think, he and I trashed bars together! And I never even suspected."

"Yes, you did," Dtimun chuckled. "So did I. But they were only suspicions. I was quite proud of Komak," he added gently. "I never told him."

"He knew, all the same." She looked up at him with wonder. "I still can hardly believe any of this is real. It seemed so impossible just a little space of time ago that we could ever bond at all."

He smiled and touched her long, red-gold hair. "I, too, never imagined this result. We have come quite a long way together since we united two warring military factions at *Ahkmau* and became the Morcai Battalion."

"And we still have at least a century to go, if everything goes as Komak thought it would."

"A century or more." He rubbed his cheek against hers.

She sighed and smiled at her mate and then at her child. "I had Edris make a vid of Rognan and Kanthor, for Komak, when he's old enough to understand how difficult it was for them to get along at all while he was on the way." She laughed at his expression. "I did explain why ancient humans boiled water and hit the baby on the bottom."

He chuckled. "They will make fine playmates for him, when he begins to walk." He glanced at her and smiled. "That will happen sooner than you imagine. Our children mature quickly."

"I've read about it. About a lot of things. I like your culture very much."

"I hoped you might," he said. "It will be a great change from military life, for you."

"Yes. But a good one."

He got to his feet and moved to the wide stone rail. "Revolution is afoot on Enmehkmehk," he said. "I think Chan Ho has very little time left to command the Rojok empire."

"I think the same."

He turned and looked at her. "The war must end soon, so that one of Komak's godfathers can step on Memcache without risking arrest and execution. My sister will rejoice on that day."

She smiled. She and Lyceria had grown close. "I'll rejoice for her, as well. Old Mardol looked as if he'd won a lottery," she added gleefully. "We owe him our lives. I'm glad he's happy here."

"He has a good heart. His stories will amuse Komak when he is old enough to hear them."

"He made vids of us, he said. Komak, I mean."

"I am certain that he picked the most embarrassing situations to record," he murmured with a grimace.

"It would be like him," she agreed.

"Are you coming inside now?" Sfilla called from the doorway. "The emperor and empress and Princess Lyceria are coming to eat with us."

"I forgot. Sorry." Madeline got up with Komak tight in her arms and walked beside Dtimun back into the house.

He let her go in first.

"I do outrank you now, don't I?" she teased. "You're standing aside for me."

He leaned down. "I outrank you," he argued. "But I give you precedence because you are carrying the heir to the throne in your arms."

"You wait," she challenged. "I'll have the best crack troop of women in the three galaxies, and they'll sing songs about me."

He chuckled. "The *kehmatemer* already do," he reminded her. "The Warwoman. Invincible."

She thought of the Latin for that word and smiled absently. Invictus. One word to describe an attitude, a credo, a pattern for living. One word to envelop all that her life had been and would be.

She pursed her lips in thought. "Invictus," she mused.

He didn't need a translation. He saw it all in her mind, like a music painting in cyberspace, such as the Cehn-Tahr designed at Kolmankash.

He studied her with quiet pride. "It is quite suitable, for such a mutinous human female," he added softly.

"At least I've stopped saluting you and calling you 'sir,'" she reminded him. And he chuckled when she gave him a wicked grin.

WITHIN THE YEAR, there were great changes in the three galaxies. Terravega had a new president, one Harmon Chakra, who swept to victory on a program of reform. The military's mental neutering policy went out the window, along with its regulations on fraternization. The government baby factories became a thing of the past. Couples of all three genders were permitted to marry and breed as they pleased. Clones were admitted to the republic as citizens and their exploitation for organ replacement was to cease. The totalitarian regimentation also ceased. All charges against the Terravegans of the Morcai Battalion were dropped and the humans were offered citizenship again.

To a man, or woman if Lieutenant Commander Edris Mallory were to be counted, they refused. Their Cehn-Tahr citizenship had become a thing of great pride, and none of the crew wished to return to Terravega. At least, as Holt Stern whispered amusedly, not until they were certain that the new rules of law were going to last longer than a few standard weeks. Stern and Hahnson, who were both clones of their originals, had a great deal more to lose than the rest of the crew if they returned to Trimerius and the clone restrictions were reinstituted. It was a new start for humanity. But most new things had growing pains. The Morcai Battalion's human faction decided to play a waiting game.

Meanwhile, Captain Rhemun was making a slow start as commander of the Morcai Battalion. He and the crew were on shaky ground. He had little to do with humans until Madeline Ruszel came along, and his prejudices against them were deep and of long duration. Lieutenant Commander Edris Mallory was having more problems with him than the rest of the crew put together. Her clumsiness and slow reactions were getting her reprimands. Even with the changes in military governance, one law was still on the books—that of three strikes and reboot. Only intimate members of the medical corps knew what that meant. It was one of the best kept military secrets, to which even the new president of Terravega was not privy. Even with their Cehn-Tahr citizenship, Edris could fall victim to Terravegan military law if the Holconcom renewed their association with the Tri-Galaxy Fleet, which was rumored to be in the offing as territorial disputes escalated in the New Territory. Dr. Strick Hahnson knew Mallory's situation, but he was reluctant to share details of it with Rhemun, who was becoming her worst enemy.

The war was beginning to wind down. A revolution had taken place on Enmehkmehk, which left Chan Ho in exile and Chacon as new party chairman and leader of the Rojok empire. It was now called the Rojok Republic, however, and rumors were flying of a liaison of some sort with the Cehn-Tahr Empire, which would result in peace.

Madeline Ruszel took all this news in her customary calm manner, smiling with each new tidbit of change and nodding complacently. She knew, as many of her confidants did not, that peace was not only a possibility, it was a certainty.

She sat down in a chair with Komak in her arms and looked down into his wide, intelligent little face. "One day in the not too distant future, I'll tell you all about how you and Mommy wrecked bars and defended the honor of the Holconcom," she whispered wickedly.

"Shame, telling the boy such stories," Dtimun scoffed as he joined her. But his eyes were green, and laughing.

"I'm preparing him so he won't be shocked when the time comes," she chuckled. She looked up at him with wide, soft eyes. "What a long way we've come from Terramer."

He nodded. He reached down and smoothed the already thick black hair on his son's head. "It has been a journey with many surprises."

"Is Chacon making the announcement soon?" she asked.

He smiled. "Tomorrow."

"There will be shock and awe in the governments of the Tri-Galaxy Council," she predicted.

"Especially when he announces the candidacy of the Rojok Republic to become a member."

"I hope they have medical personnel standing by to administer stimulants," she said.

He dropped down elegantly into a chair across from her. "The emperor has a gift."

"For me?"

He nodded. "They are recruiting for the first corps of female military candidates. You yourself will choose those who gain membership to the elite group."

She caught her breath. "How kind of him!"

"He is quite fond of you."

She smiled, happy in her new relations. And her mate. She looked down at the baby. "Did you hear that? Mommy is a brigadier general. She's going to lead armies one day."

Dtimun was recalling what Komak had told him about the future—that Madeline led a division of female troops and sneaked out to go on missions with them when she was much older. He chuckled.

"Why are you laughing?" she wondered.

"A stray thought. And no, I will not share it. Not yet." He got up, bent and kissed them both. "I must attend yet another planning session for the upcoming nuptials. At least two members of our household will faint when they learn that the Cehn-Tahr princess is to wed a Rojok general."

"Premier of the Rojok Republic," she corrected.

He shrugged. He grinned. "It will be a pleasure not to have to scramble and vent every message I exchange with him."

"I'm sure Lyceria feels the same way."

"Changes. So many changes," he mused. "And at the center of them, a redheaded physician with a hot temper and a wicked sense of humor. I would never have expected such a catalyst."

"I would never have expected it, either. Or an end to the war." She frowned. "How will we learn to live in a peaceful universe?" she wondered aloud.

"There will always be wars," he said complacently. "But small ones, I hope, after this."

She nodded. She smiled up at him warmly. "Caneese and I have a new project. We're using a derivative of the secretion the Nagaashe contributed to study its effect on time dilation theory in her Coswerp Chamber. Acceleration of biological cells in magnetic suspension with emerillium bursts to displace time."

He didn't say it, but he had a sneaking suspicion that this research would one day lead to Komak's ability to jump through dimensions and timelines, as the Nagaashe and the galots were able to.

"An interesting hypothesis."

"It is, isn't it? Basically it would cause time to distort and shift, rather than requiring the person affected to do the shifting." She frowned. "Caneese is brilliant."

"She is, but your liaison with the Nagaashe has provided the element that was missing from her experiments."

"The gland that has tissue no biochemist can replicate," she agreed.

A chime sounded. He glanced at his communicator ring. "A signal that I am expected, and late."

"Do you miss leading the Holconcom?" she asked abruptly, and seemed to hang on his answer.

He smoothed back her hair. "We are still on active duty. In the future it is quite possible that we may be in the vanguard of some new offensive against a new enemy," he told her.

"When the children grow up," she agreed.

He bent and smoothed his cheek against hers. "In the meanwhile," he murmured, "it might be as well to keep up your martial arts practice." He hesitated. "Not with Flannegan," he added coldly.

She was amused. Flannegan had actually dropped in to congratulate them on the birth of their son, from a cautious distance. Dtimun's reaction had been quite noticeable and Flannegan had not stayed long.

"Or with Rhemun," he added, and the sound was like a growl.

"I'll do my sparring with you," she promised.

He shifted uncomfortably. "This behavior should have abated after the bonding ceremony," he said.

"No need to apologize," she assured him with twinkling eyes. "If you recall, I made a rather testy comment to that Cehn-Tahr aristocrat who was a little too flirtatious with you at the christening."

It had flattered him that Madeline did not like other females touching him.

"Perhaps we should both learn to be less possessive of each other," he commented.

She looked at him, pursed her lips. Then she said, "Noooo. I don't think so."

And he burst out laughing.

"I have something for you."

"For me? What is it?"

He drew a small package from under his robes and handed it to her. He held Komak while she unwrapped the gift, delicately pulling apart the handmade cellulose paper and matching ribbon to disclose a...

"It's a book!" she exclaimed. She was fascinated. She'd never seen a book made of real cellulose and printed with ancient human language. She could read it, after a fashion, although it was slow going at first. "Why, it's a poem!"

"Yes. We discussed the term 'Invictus' and I remembered seeing this on a nexus site. I sent for a copy of it. It is a text of a poem from ancient Earth which survived many catastrophes." The poem was written by a human from Great Britain, William Ernest Henley.

She opened the pages with careful hands and looked at the words. "...my head is bloody but unbowed..." she read. She glanced up at him with frank wonder. "I've never touched a real book before."

He smiled. "I thought you might enjoy it."

"I'll pass it down to Komak and teach it to him. Do the Cehn-Tahr write poetry?"

"Yes, we have poets, too. You will find many digital volumes in the library."

She gave him a droll look. "It was nice of you to finally put back the vids of newborn Cehn-Tahr children so that I could see what they looked like."

He grinned. "You did not know what I looked like at the time. I had no wish to frighten you," he said as he laid the baby gently in her arms.

"I don't recall ever wearing a short skirt and running away screaming from a space monster," she pointed out.

"I would pity the space monster," he teased. "It is he who would run away screaming."

"You got that right," she asserted. She looked down

at the small, precious book, shifting her son so that he lay in the crook of her arm. "Thank you."

"You are quite welcome. And please refrain from educating our son about future bar brawls in which he will participate," he added firmly.

She wrinkled her nose at him. "Don't start, or I'll salute you at the next ceremonial function," she threatened.

He shook his head, sighed, and walked out with regal grace. But he was smiling.

* * * * *

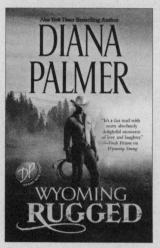

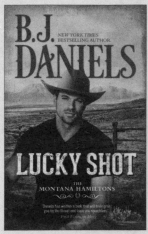

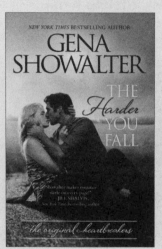

REQUEST YOUR
FREE BOOKS!

2 FREE NOVELS
FROM THE SUSPENSE COLLECTION
PLUS 2 FREE GIFTS!

YES! Please send me 2 FREE novels from the Suspense Collection and my 2 FREE gifts (gifts are worth about $10). After receiving them, if I don't wish to receive any more books, I can return the shipping statement marked "cancel." If I don't cancel, I will receive 4 brand-new novels every month and be billed just $6.49 per book in the U.S. or $6.99 per book in Canada. That's a savings of at least 19% off the cover price. It's quite a bargain! Shipping and handling is just 50¢ per book in the U.S. and 75¢ per book in Canada.* I understand that accepting the 2 free books and gifts places me under no obligation to buy anything. I can always return a shipment and cancel at any time. Even if I never buy another book, the two free books and gifts are mine to keep forever.

191/391 MDN GH4Z

Name	(PLEASE PRINT)	
Address		Apt. #
City	State/Prov.	Zip/Postal Code

Signature (if under 18, a parent or guardian must sign)

Mail to the **Reader Service:**
IN U.S.A.: P.O. Box 1867, Buffalo, NY 14240-1867
IN CANADA: P.O. Box 609, Fort Erie, Ontario L2A 5X3

Want to try two free books from another line?
Call 1-800-873-8635 or visit www.ReaderService.com.